# BOOKS BY M K SCOTT

*Cupid's Catering Company*
Culinary Cozy Mystery

Wedding Cake Blues
Truffle Me Not
Double Chocolate Deception

*The Talking Dog Detective Agency*
Cozy Mystery

A Bark in the Night
Requiem for a Rescue Dog Queen
Bark Twice for Danger
The Ghostly Howl
Dog Park Romeo
On St. Nick's Trail

*The Painted Lady Inn Mysteries Series*
Culinary Cozy Mystery

Murder Mansion
Drop Dead Handsome
Killer Review
Christmas Calamity

Death Pledges a Sorority
Caribbean Catastrophe
Weddings Can be Murder
The Skeleton Wore Diamonds
Death of a Honeymoon
Cakewalk to Murder
Sailors Take Warning
Two Many Sleuths (Oct 2021)

*The Way Over the Hill Gang Series*
Cozy Mystery

Late for Dinner
Late for Bingo
Late for Shuffleboard
Late for Square Dancing
Late for Love
Late for the Wedding (Dec 2021)

# DOUBLE CHOCOLATE DECEPTION

## By
## M K Scott

# CHAPTER ONE

L IVING WITH A detective father taught Della that life could spiral out of control at any moment. Many urgent police calls shelved dinner plans, a vacation, and even his attendance at her school play. It couldn't be helped. Somewhere in Owens, someone else experienced something much worse than their father missing a high school play where the daughter had at the most two lines.

Her ever cheerful mother sat across from her, nursing her cup of coffee in the dimly lit bakery while gossiping about her neighbors. Somehow, her mother's armor of good intentions protected her from the arrows that life threw, including the abrupt death of her husband—or at least that's the appearance she gave. Mabel Delacroix could serve as a poster child for rolling with the punches.

Della considered herself the type of gal who always waited for the next boot to drop. Often, when events snowballed into an ever-increasing mass of improbable, unfortunate mishaps, she'd sometimes think *what else could happen?* Even on a good day, she often worried it wouldn't last. In that regard, life never disappointed.

Loud knocking rattled the glass bakery door. Della froze, uncertain what to do. They were closed on Sundays. If she ignored her insistent rapper, maybe they'd leave since the CLOSED sign wasn't working. To meet in the café area where everyone could see them through the windows was probably a mistake, but ignoring a potential customer was the kind of thing that'd spread around town like wildfire.

In her short experience, no one with good news showed up before the sun arrived. Her mother had no such hesitation. She left her chair and opened the door. "My goodness, Clarice. What's wrong? You're never running around this early on your day off."

The red-faced woman staggered into the room, glancing over one shoulder as if looking for someone before closing the door. Clarice rested against the door as she exhaled. "I need your help. I remember you saying you'd be here this morning."

"Birthday cake? Unexpected party to cater?" Della queried, alarmed at her mother's friend's appearance. It had to be a pressing need for her to show up at seven in the morning. "Do you need a box of pastries?" She pushed to her feet and headed toward the kitchen. There should be enough leftovers to make a box. If not, she could pop a tray of goodies into the oven.

"Oh no! That's not it." She fanned her face with her hand. "Not sure if it's the aggravation of everything that's happened or another darn hot flash. I need your and your mom's sleuthing skills."

Della stopped in her tracks and pivoted. "What?"

The exclamation hadn't rattled her mother. She guided her friend to a seat and picked up a paper tablet and a pen from the counter. "What was the instigating incident?" Mabel flipped open the tablet and the pen hovered above the paper.

Instigating incident? Della slid into a nearby chair and managed not to snort. Who talked like that? Certainly not her father, who had spoken to people in a conversational style. She'd commented more than once how he favored the small-town inspectors so popular in the BBC mysteries. Somehow, they managed to convey civility and curiosity when questioning a suspect. Her mother must be quoting someone from a favorite crime drama.

All the same, what could have upset Clarice? Mabel often joked her friend's thick skin could deflect a sharp knife. The foolhardy attacker would then be left vulnerable to Clarice's rapier tongue.

Due to cradling her head in her hands, Clarice's reply sounded more like a sound puzzle with not enough right pieces to form a sentence.

Her mother nudged her friend gently. "We're going to need a little more than that to go on."

Clarice lifted her head and said, "Something weird is happening." She paused and shook her head. "My life is going south big time."

Talk about no help at all. Who hadn't uttered the same words after making a social gaffe, wrecking a car, losing a job, or being served with divorce papers? As the biggest gossip in town, Clarice cared little about appropriate social behavior so that couldn't be it. As a happy divorcée, the end of a relationship fizzled as a possibility.

"How is your life going south?" Mabel asked as she put down the pad and pen to lightly rub circles on her friend's back. "Last we talked, you had a tropical getaway planned."

For some reason, back circles calmed a person, or at least it worked on Clarice, who sniffed and then cleared her throat. "The signs were there, but I pooh-poohed them as a mistake or a clever angle by a salesman."

She was still not making sense, but Della would leave it to her mother to extract information. Even her father had joked that they needed her at the station just to sit in the waiting area and casually chit-chat with the suspects to obtain needed details.

"What salesman?" Her mother shot Della a look and pushed the tablet toward her. Okay, it must mean she got to scribe. *Salesman?* Della wrote, adding a question mark.

"The Mercedes salesman. He wanted to know if I had decided on a color for the convertible. Then later, I got another call from the BMW dealership. They all went to my voicemail, and I never returned their calls, but what's the possibility of getting two calls from two high-end car dealerships in one day? They said my name in the call and acted as if I'd been on the lot."

Mabel shot her friend a questioning look, causing Clarice to straighten up while firming her jaw. She tossed her head, making her short locks tremble. "You think I don't remember going to a car dealership? I'd know if I had. Besides, I love my little car. It's easy on the car mileage, fun to drive, and I can always snag a parking space. Why would I go buying an expensive car? I wouldn't. I have to save for my retirement since there is only one of me to provide for my golden years."

"I know." Mabel lifted her brows in Della's direction. It was a signal of sorts, but no one bothered mentioning what it meant. When in doubt, offer food.

"Clarice, would you like a hot cheese Danish? How about a cup of coffee?"

The woman patted her stomach and grimaced. "I'm watching my weight." When Della sat motionlessly, Clarice added, "It's been a rough day, and it's not even eight. I guess one cheese Danish wouldn't hurt. If you have any chocolate croissants, get me one of those, too."

Not wanting to miss any of the story, Della vaulted from her chair and rushed into the kitchen to grab the desired goodies and warm them up a tad. The treats on a plate, she approached the table in time to hear Clarice say, "I can't imagine anyone who would have it out for me."

Seriously, the woman gathered juicy gossip in her post-op recovery nurse job while patients mumbled names other than their spouses or children. Mabel confided a few even mentioned shady business deals while shaking off the effects of the anesthesia. It made her wonder if guilt weighed on them so much it was at the forefront of their minds while possibly worried they might die, and everything would come out. Even though Clarice bragged no one could trace any gossip back to her, Della suspected a few did. Who knows what damage a few murmured words under anesthesia might cause if the wrong person got wind of it?

Della placed the plate in front of Clarice. "I'll get your coffee, but I'll need to know everything you told Mom while I was in the kitchen."

A long sigh answered the request, and Clarice managed a weary smile. "Could I have coffee first? I haven't had any. Went to the gas station and my ATM card didn't work. Went inside to pay because sometimes cards don't work at the pump. She ran my card but told me it was no good." Clarice pressed her hand against her chest. "She implied I had no money in the bank. Me. No money. Thank goodness, I had my emergency twenty in my wallet. Something's up." She gulped hard and continued. "I have a standing order at Bill's Donuts."

At the mention of one of her competitors, Della narrowed her eyes in Clarice's direction. The donut shop located near the highway didn't offer a sitting area, lattes, or breakfast sandwiches.

"Oh please! Don't take that attitude with me. I changed your diaper more than a few times." She grimaced before continuing. "Not pleasant. Anyhow, you're not open on Sundays. Because I'm usually in a hurry, I prepaid for my coffee and bran muffin monthly. Only today, I gave a new employee my name, and she just gives me this dull stare. She tells me I've already been by."

"A mistake?" Mabel suggested gently but gave Della the side-eye to make sure she wrote every word down. Caught up in the story, Della picked up the pen and did her best to catch up.

"Not sure. So many slightly-off things have been happening. One is a fluke. Two feels peculiar. Three means something is wrong, big time."

"What's the third?" Della glanced up from writing to ask.

Clarice sighed heavily and took an aggressive bite out of her cheese Danish. A cow out in the field meditatively chewing its cud might be a trifle faster than Clarice. Della and Mabel waited while the woman chewed slowly.

Finally, she spoke. "My tropical cruise was canceled. Every morning I get up and pull up the website to enjoy the day-to-day countdown, dreaming a little about the warm water and white sand beaches. Today, there was no cruise listed. No customer service either to answer my questions."

Yeah, it did sound suspicious, but there could be a reasonable explanation for everything. Della waved her pen, ready to explain. "Sometimes, *I* have trouble at the pump using my credit card. The clerk at the place didn't know how to run your card. A new clerk at the donut shop, embarrassed she gave away your order, insisted you were there." She paused to make sure Clarice knew she sacrificed service by frequenting Bill's. "As you probably know, all older women resemble each other."

Both Clarice and her mother snorted at her theory. Della, not discouraged, plowed ahead. "Younger people think everyone over thirty looks about the same. As for your trip, it could be a problem with the website. Your cruise may appear when you look at the website later."

Looking unconvinced, Clarice drummed her fingernails on the table and nodded in Mabel's direction.

Her mother cleared her throat. "After thinking this over…"

Della expected her mother to pretty much echo her own words and possibly, because her friend had said it, Clarice would accept it. With no reason to write anymore, Della put down the pen and folded her arms, wanting to see Clarice's reaction.

"I'm certain something is up. What I'm uncertain about is if someone is trying to annoy you or hijack your life."

# CHAPTER TWO

ELLA'S MOUTH DROPPED open. She turned to stare at her mother. Silhouetted by the rising sun, it was difficult to discern her expression, but her answer about someone trying to assume Clarice's identity reminded Della more of a pod person sci-fi movie. Would there be pods for both her and her mother ripening in the storeroom? Surely the idea would pull a giggle from Clarice.

Somber faced, the woman stroked her chin. "I don't know, Mabel. It's a possibility, but not sure who'd want to be me. It's not like I have a movie star lifestyle. The coffee and bran muffin are pretty much the highlights of my day."

What? Della glanced between her mother and friend with the realization they were very serious. She held both hands up. "Hijack? Isn't that a little over the top? The other day I went to get gas and my credit card wouldn't work." Remembering the incident also resurrected the smidgen of panic she'd felt, certain she'd overdrawn her account. "Then, I looked down at my card and noticed the teeth marks where Tony, Mother's new canine companion, chewed on it."

"Hey, now," her mother added with a slight chin lift, "you should know by now if you leave your purse on the floor it is fair game."

"I don't have any dog chewed credit cards." Clarice shot a hand through her short coiffure. "Not sure what to do first. Should I call up the credit card agencies? Freeze my credit with the various credit agencies? Notify the local police?"

Mabel nodded. "I'd do everything, but probably call the credit card companies first. Someone could be charging a boatload of iguana supplies or indulging with designer duds on your nickel. The real question is, do they want your credit, or do they want to be you?"

Instead of answering, Clarice polished off the chocolate croissant in two major bites. Sure, the pastry packed a bit of air, but two bites for a normal size croissant? Someone needed comfort food majorly. In the freezer, an uncut pumpkin praline cheesecake waited for Monday. It might not make it until tomorrow.

"Could I get you anything else?"

Clarice smiled at Della. "Would you? It's Sunday, you know. No banks, no credit bureaus, no credit card agencies will be open today."

"Not true," Mabel assured her, reaching across the table to pat her friend's hand. "Banks will be closed, but you can call the credit card agencies and possibly go online for the bureaus. People are always losing their cards." She caught Della's eye. "No more sugar. We need some real food. Isn't there some turkey or pastrami left from the super sub you made for the birthday party?"

There was no need to tell Della twice. She might as well assemble the sandwich with some fresh veggies. Here she thought this morning would be a brainstorming session on how to get Cupid's Catering Company into people's minds and keep her out of the red. An article she read on new restaurants mentioned they needed five years of income in the bank to survive before they built up their clientele to survive on their own. It might be the same for bakeries.

Unfortunately, no five-year cash cushion existed to keep her afloat.

A frantic Clarice had Mabel basically dropping everything to deal with her drama. Not to sound uncaring, but this wasn't the first time Clarice insisted everyone stop their lives because she had an issue. The singles mixer Clarice had talked her mother into enrolling herself and Della into attending, in exchange for the privilege of catering it, came to mind. Despite the money they paid, neither of them participated in the meet and greet. As for helping them with the work involved, as Clarice promised—that didn't happen, either.

Inside the kitchen, Della opened the fridge, extracted the needed items, and carried them to the kitchen island. Presentation mattered even if you were just making a comfort sandwich to soak up all the sugar. She sliced open one of the sourdough buns she got from Burgers, Brews, and Books as part of a food trade. Guy, the owner— who happened to be cute in a nerdy chic kind of way with glasses, curly hair, and a crooked smile—baked fabulous buns. Her cookies rocked, which resulted in exchanging cookies for buns while promoting one another.

Her mother gave a broad wink and made kissy sounds whenever Guy's name came up—totally immature and inaccurate. At best, they were friends and business associates. No kissing had ever happened and probably wouldn't. Not that she'd be opposed, but she wouldn't make the mistake of thinking a relationship existed between them other than friendship. Too many women did that, thinking hanging out equaled happily ever after. Before they knew it, they were imagining what their future children would look like and deciding if Jamaica or Fiji would be the better honeymoon destination.

Not her. She'd not make that mistake. It was better for her to be a friend, rather than some needy chick that writers apparently loved to satirize in movies. Besides, she could use another friend.

Knowing Clarice's preferences, Della slathered mayonnaise on the bun. Her lips firmed into a narrow line as she considered the woman visiting Bill's Donut Shop. Sure, he had donuts and she didn't, but she'd put good money on his bran muffins being store-bought. As for the theory of someone trying to be Clarice, it didn't work. She could accept that someone might want to tie into her good credit rating or create a series of new credit cards with Clarice's name while going to a new address. For all she knew, someone could have a fake ID with Clarice's name, but that could be sloppy.

According to her father, fake IDs usually sold anywhere from three hundred to a thousand dollars then and probably have gone up since he passed away. For the lower priced ones, you got what you got, which usually was someone who didn't look a bit like you for a picture ID. A red-headed guy with freckles might obtain a driver's license for Krishna Patel. For the more expensive IDs, they took pictures of the purchaser and were able to create sophisticated documents, complete with watermarks. They weren't foolproof. Most of those nabbed were entering nightclubs or buying liquor. They usually ended up on probation and paying a minor fine, although it was not enough to persuade a young person that being older equaled more fun.

Her nose crinkled as she wondered what happened to those kids who wanted to seem older.

Her father mentioned that most of the names came from dead people. It was easy enough to get their names from gravestones, then buy birth certificates online with the appropriate information. Live people tended to complain, rather like Clarice, when someone showed up with their name. All the same, there had to be a lot of the same names with so many people in the world. Probably only one Della Delacroix in the world, though. Any other parent would have spotted the similarity between the first and last name.

Sandwich finished with turkey and a slice of Swiss, she added carrot and red pepper strips. A small box on the counter held tiny country flags she'd purchased for an around the world dinner she'd catered. Picking one at random, she stuck it in the sandwich.

Tiny umbrellas made drinks more fun. It followed little flags should do the same for sandwiches. Plate in hand, she backed into the swinging door and schooled her face into moderate concern. No need for Clarice or her mother to know she had doubts about someone trying to take Clarice's place. On that account, she'd side with Clarice on not having a life worth wanting.

Besides, over the years, it hadn't escaped her notice how adults could act like big kids. As kids went, Clarice always needed more attention than most, which explained the gossip. Apparently, not many people could resist a gossipy tidbit.

Odd happenings clumped together might look like a chain of events but weren't necessarily related. A car dealership could get a list of homeowners from public records and possibly their phone numbers. Then they call the homeowners asking which color convertible they'd prefer. It could get someone who hadn't been considering it before thinking about a jazzy new car.

An email from a car dealership about a utility van almost gave Della heart palpitations since it had started out *Congrats on your purchase of a smart cargo vehicle!* It sounded as if she had somehow purchased one in her sleep. Maybe the same thing had happened with Clarice but two in the same day did smell weird. Then again, they could be buying their mailing lists from the same company.

"Here's your sandwich!" she sang out as she approached the table.

Her hope that they'd moved on to a different topic vanished when Clarice grabbed the tiny flag and waved it. "Russian! That's got to be it. They have some sort of white slave ring with Russian girls. They must have one pretending to be me."

The tiny little flag with the red, white, and blue stripes and a heraldic emblem belonged to Slovakia. Della chose not to mention it, along with the inability of twenty-year-old Russian girls to pass themselves off as sixty-year-old Midwestern women. *Not everything you think needs to come out of your mouth* may have been one of her father's better quotes.

Now, if she could only get back to coming up with a creative idea to keep her business in the black. Maybe Clarice could help. If nothing else, she reigned as one of Owens' most creative thinkers, due to how she embellished the facts.

# CHAPTER THREE

A WHITE FACE with oversized blue eyebrows stared back from the mirror. Della crinkled her nose. The image did the same. She picked up a red lip liner pencil in preparation for drawing on a huge, fake smile. "I'm not sure why I have to be the clown. You know how I feel about clowns."

"Someone who doesn't like clowns." Her mother shook her head. "You had to be the only child who cried when the clowns made their appearance in the circus ring."

A long hiss sounded from the air compressor as Mabel blew up a long balloon for balloon animals. Making balloon animals was another skill Della passed on learning, unaware it could come in handy. Hopefully, the kids would be happy with snakes and swords.

"I didn't cry." She felt the need to point that out as she pressed the lipliner into her skin.

The smile came out lopsided as if made by a drunk clown. Great. Della placed the lip liner where the original line had gone astray and sketched out another line to make a better smile, but certainly not a perfect one. She'd be the ambivalent clown torn between laughter and tears. "If you remember, I complained."

"How could I forget?" Her mother pulled a balloon off the air compressor and tied it in crisp, neat movements. "When is this going to be over? I'm bored. The clowns are stupid."

"Can you blame me? Even at a young age, I understood the job of the clown was to distract people from act changes. They were simply filler."

"Entertainers."

"For some."

"For many. There were plenty of children who enjoyed the clown act. In their eyes, the clown is a celebrity. Keep that in mind when we go to the Anderson birthday party. Thank goodness Elise is coming by to help."

The thought of her ever-resourceful high school helper gave Della an idea, a perfectly marvelous one. "Elise could be the clown. She'd be good at it."

"Not today. Good try, trying to get out of it." Her mother chortled. Often in the act of merriment, her mother laughed so hard she ended up making herself laugh even more. This happened to be one of those times. Her hand rested on the kitchen wall as she caught her breath. "It's all you, sweetie. Elise needs to take one of those tests for college. You know the ones that show how smart you are? If you score high enough, schools fight over you."

"SATs. Yeah, she mentioned it. I forgot about it in my excitement about my debut as a clown."

"Not surprising. Once we added clown to our birthday party package, you got five bookings."

"Whoo." Della circled her finger in the air. "I'm surprised there are five families who want clowns at their child's party. Haven't they heard of Pennywise, the evil clown?"

"Hmmm…"

Her mother pondered the possibility while giving Della's costume a once over. Her gingham dress paired with lizard skin leggings screamed fashion disaster and something no one would don intentionally.

"Those leggings might scare a few of the children. They might think you are a mutant something."

"All the better," Della teased but felt the need to clarify. "They'd like the idea I was a mutant like the various comic book heroes."

Her mother bobbed her head. "I've seen a few superhero movies. Trust me. You don't look like any of them."

"Geesh! I thought mothers were supposed to make you feel good about yourself."

"Della, you know what I mean. You're devoid of any oddities, such as laser eyes."

There was no need to add she knew exactly what her mother meant. Della was average for most purposes from height to size. Even though she often bought her clothes in the plus-size section, she realized a good portion of women did likewise. "Maybe we could do a superhero-style clown."

"I'm not sure *superhero* and *clown* go together. We might try the scary clown but only for adult parties."

Talk about an idea that didn't thrill. "One clown at a time. Let's see how *this* party goes."

Under no circumstances would Della ever pretend to be an evil clown. Even dressing as a non-violent clown put her out of her comfort zone. "What will the children expect?"

"Gags. Like chasing them around with a bucket that's filled with confetti, only they don't know it isn't water until you throw it. Dad jokes—you know the type with the punch line being a pun. Cheap gifts like glow in the dark necklaces."

"Gifts? We've already invested in an air compressor to blow up balloons. I want to make money, not spend it."

"New things need some investment. Besides, I bought the necklaces at the dollar store. Sure, there's an initial investment, but most of your costume we pulled from your roles as an extra in the school plays."

True enough. Della had pulled out the full skirt of her dress from the play *Oklahoma*. Her red, pigtailed wig waited on a wig head, courtesy of *Pippi Longstocking* from grade school. Fortunately, she had a big head even in grade school, which allowed her to still wear the wig. A person might think she'd had the lead role in that particular play. She did not. Instead, a thwarted drama teacher created a chorus of Pippi Longstockings, who often repeated whatever the main actor said in a louder, more annoying tone. It resembled Pippi Meets Electra—the Greek Tragedy Electra, as opposed to the one known for her pipes and her legs. A pair of bright yellow rain boots from *Singing in the Rain* completed the outfit.

"You're right. I guess I was hoping more for the city council to bite at the downtown Mardi Gras event idea. That would end up with me making beignets, king cake, and leaving the jelly donuts to Bill's Donuts. We might even convince Guy to offer shrimp creole, jambalaya, or shrimp and grits at his restaurant."

"Well..." Her mother lengthened the word, giving her head a shake as she continued. "If anyone could convince him, I'm sure it would be you. Keep in mind, his place is known for burgers and beer. Hence the name, Burgers, Brews, and Books."

"You're right. No reason I can't put together some king cakes, though. You'd think the council would jump at something to put a little color in the dreary winter months after Christmas."

"Maybe next year," her mother suggested with a wink. "Only you need to get other merchants on board with it. Consider a way each business can be involved. Food is a natural, but what else could the other merchants offer?"

Coming up with an event-appropriate special might be up to the other shopkeepers. There was not much she could think of for Thomas' Taxidermist or the Clock Store. "You're right. I guess I was trying to hurry things. Didn't have proper time to plan with Clarice bursting into our planning session and melting down. How is she, by the way?"

"About the same, although her accounts are frozen to prevent any new accounts started in her name."

"That's good." Even though she knew she'd probably regret saying anything, Della chose to ask the unspoken question as she penciled in her lip area consuming the bottom half of her face. Maybe her clown persona veered toward blabbermouth. "Do you think anything *really* happened to Clarice?"

No need to tack on *was it all for attention?* That part her mother understood. "Hard to say. She did finally reach the cruise customer service and found out her trip had been canceled in lieu of an Alaskan cruise."

Going someplace where cold drinks with tiny umbrellas weren't served by handsome cabana boys in Hawaiian shirts didn't sound like Clarice's usual getaway. "That doesn't sound like her."

"I know," her mother agreed and pointed to a spot beside her natural lips. "You need to fill that in. Anyhow, Clarice wasn't pleased and insisted she hadn't changed her reservations and insisted they change them back." She folded her arms and rolled her eyes. "I can imagine Clarice seething and calling them incompetent before transforming into a crying mess."

"Clarice? Cry?" Talk about unlikely but she could be very touchy about her vacations. "Did it work?"

Mabel shrugged her shoulders and busied herself by picking up filled balloons and putting them into a basket. "Must have. They changed her reservation back, but her special cabin got gobbled up by someone else. I'm just thankful she managed to get back on the cruise. We'd never hear the end of it if she hadn't."

Even though she knew Clarice loved to be in the limelight, something didn't sit right with her about the cruise being changed. "Was the cruise Clarice got switched to cheaper?"

"I haven't a clue," her mother answered. "Now, you need a clown name. How about Daffy Della?"

"No! I don't want anyone to know it's me behind the makeup. Besides, that's what one of the primary school mean girls used to call me. Maybe something elegant like Petal."

Her mother stuck out her tongue and pretended to gag. "Awful. No pizazz. We need something to make the kids smile. How about Droopy Drawers? However, most of the kids wouldn't get that. How about Droopy Pants?"

"I'm wearing a dress." Who knew she'd actually be grateful for her ugly gingham dress? She pulled at the waist—not because it strained against her stomach but just the opposite. It felt looser than before. "I need a girl's name like Sassy."

"That's a cat's name. How about Giggles? Glitterbug, Freckles, or Penny Pincher? You could carry around a giant penny and pretend to make it scream."

"Freckles will work. I just need to add a few." Della sharpened the eyebrow pencil in preparation for freckles.

Mabel plucked the pencil from Della's hand. "Too much of a delicate touch. No one will see those freckles. You've got to go big as a clown. Splashy. Loud. Over the top."

"I suppose," Della half-heartedly agreed, but her mind stayed with the same subject. "Do you think someone did switch her reservation? Why would they?"

Her mother stopped drawing tiny circles on Della's face and placed one fisted hand on her hip. "Clarice and I went to grade school together. She hasn't changed a great deal. Over the years, she's ruffled a few feathers. Someone being mad at her wouldn't surprise me. I don't know that they could get her information about the cruise, though. Maybe it could have been lifted from a computer. Maybe she looked up her cruise at work and accidentally left the website up."

"Possibly," Della agreed, not wanting to think of anyone in Owens being that mean-spirited. "I'd rather think it was a mistake, but it just wasn't something minor like scheduling Clarice for the wrong dinner time. It was an entirely different cruise. One had to be canceled, which I'm sure customer reps try to discourage, and then another one booked. Any decent rep would have tried to talk her into two cruises."

"Sounds about right, but I'm not mentioning it." Mabel's head swung side to side with vigor. She returned to drawing freckles on her daughter's face. "If someone hates Clarice that much to cause trouble for her, I'm not pointing it out. If so, I suspect she knows who it is. Anything I say will just be embarrassing."

# CHAPTER FOUR

E MPTY PIZZA BOXES littered the dining room table and perfumed the air with a heavy bite of tangy tomato sauce and melted cheese. Della wearied of telling her dad jokes badly, and that was a stretch. The very nature of a dad joke usually relied on an obvious word pun. It usually aimed for the primary school set with gems like what type of suitcases do elephants use for vacation, with the answer being trunks. Elephants pack their trunks for traveling. When the listeners failed to recognize the pun initially, it didn't help to explain it. The wall served as her sanctuary out of the path of rampaging partiers. There was a good chance the mother might have settled for a grocery store bought cake if Della hadn't put up the promotion for birthday clowns per her mother's advice. Even though she considered the idea of clowns showing up at parties a dated concept, it had snagged her an order for a cupcake cake in the shape of a dinosaur.

Childish shrieks sounded as a young girl dressed in snowflake leggings and a T-shirt chased the birthday boy, waving her balloon sword menacingly while yelling, "I'm going to kill you!"

A sharp look from the mother, party planner, and bill payer in Della's direction meant she should do something—not sure why she would think that. Peace negotiator and security guard never figured into clowning. Running feet and shrieking continued up the stairs, a plus since they'd be out of sight. Still, she should probably do something if she wanted referrals to future parties.

On her arrival earlier, one child had shouted clowns were stupid. Even though Della may have agreed on one level, to say so ranked as super rude. Another darling stomped on her feet to see if her shoes squeaked. Apparently, some clowns' shoes *do* squeak. Even though her big toe still throbbed, she assured herself it couldn't be broken.

Twenty-odd second graders cooped up in an overheated house smelled like disaster. Bet the mother didn't expect them all to show up. Add in copious amounts of sugar, boredom, and a low skills clown and you have one incredibly long Saturday for everyone. A common myth about clowns was they were often sad, suffering from depression, and had occasional drinking issues. If this served as their day-to-day life, Della felt for the costumed entertainers.

A petite blonde girl trotted up to Della and beamed. She stuck her hand out in greeting. How sweet! Thankfully, some of the children had learned manners. Why couldn't they all be like this? At least she'd have the memory of one, precious, well-behaved child that would keep her going. Della held out her hand to the pint-sized princess with the party tiara balanced on her curls.

"How are you, sweetheart?"

Della's gloved hand closed over the much smaller one only to feel a small zap and hear a buzz. The girl giggled before jerking her hand away and running off. Well, that explained where her hand buzzer ended up. The bag of gags her mother thought appropriate for the party, including a flower corsage that sprayed people, a hand buzzer, a laughing box, and a whoopee cushion vanished as soon as Della put them down on the counter. The whoopee cushion made an appearance when the birthday boy's nana sat down to an embarrassing farting sound. The red-faced woman murmured *pardon me* but treated the party participants to a knowing survey.

Hopefully, the attendees would carry the blame for the gags. As for the confetti-filled bucket, the client shot her a horrified stare as the colorful debris landed on the sand-colored Berber carpeting. If the homeowner wanted to keep her home pristine, she should have opted elsewhere for the party, such as a bowling alley, a children's pizza parlor, or even one of those activity centers where the children work out their energy by climbing through tunnels and jumping into ball pits.

Della would much prefer such a scenario with the children all busy climbing or jumping. They would be too busy to harass the clown. She sighed heavily, but anyone who coughed over the money for a party at such a place would have little left to hire a clown. Until she donned the ridiculous wig, no clowns existed in Owens. It was very curious. Growing up there had been many clowns in parades. Even some men's organization members dressed up as clowns and gave out balloons. A half-dozen drove tiny cars in the parades, which she had to admit rocked, especially the figure-eight pattern.

Movement of the adult kind registered in Della's peripheral vision, and she pivoted to greet Elise. Smiling as her headband, complete with spring-attached ladybugs, swayed and bounced, she at least *acted* happy.

Her smile dropped when she reached Della. "Your mother sent me."

"Of course she did." For a woman who wanted grandchildren, she had managed to vanish.

To excuse her absence, Mabel would point out that her grandchildren would be well-behaved. Della rocked up on her toes and peered around her employee, whose expression shifted into a cross between anxious and possibly fearful.

"Where is dear Mama?"

"Well," Elise started and cleared her throat, "she's on the front porch with the grandmother and her daughter, having a nice chat. They're both super nice."

Winter had settled into the Midwest with a vengeance, with daytime temperatures never climbing above thirty. Dirty snow created its own guard rails on the road and parking lots contained icy mountains of cleared snow. The picture-postcard moment of winter ended about twelve hours after the season officially started. Most Midwesterners just endured the cold, regretting they had neither the money nor the opportunity to head south as so many snowbirds did.

"It's freezing out there."

"It is," Elise acknowledged and chafed her arms as if remembering. "But it is quiet and calm on the porch."

It sounded as if Elise might have taken refuge on the porch, too. "Mother sent you in on a mission. I suspect you didn't volunteer."

The employee dropped her chin and murmured something inaudible. Frenzied barking occurred as a large terrier zoomed around children. It was hard to say if the dog was joining in the festivities or objected to them. The beleaguered mother joined in the chase, demanding to know who let the dog out. Did it matter who the culprit was? On the second time around, Della deftly grabbed the dog's collar. The winded mother accepted control of the terrier and ferried it off down the hall. Elise stared hard at the woman, which made no sense.

Della angled her head in the direction of the departing woman. "You got an issue with her?"

"Not until her payment came up as not sufficient funds. Mabel wanted you to know so you could shake her down for the money before we left."

A mental image of her flipping over the much taller woman and shaking her until enough money fell out to cover the sweets and clown appearance flashed through her head. She was not sure what her mother expected her to do. "Could it be a mistake?"

"I doubt it. Grandma was on the porch. She overheard our discussion and decided to weigh in. She mentioned her daughter-in-law had never been much of a money manager. The daughter, Kathy, who was there, too, commented. She works at the bank and said she'd received many panicked phone calls to check on her sister-in-law's account and a few times to float her a loan because, after all, they were family."

"Anyhow," Elise continued, "Grandma pointed out that her son's working abroad for the time being and finances were left in the daughter-in-law's less than reliable hands. Could be she didn't bother to balance her checkbook. People do that."

"Yes, they do." Della found herself agreeing. This wasn't the first time she'd been stiffed. At least it wasn't a huge event. What surprised her was the family's willingness to talk about a family issue to practically everyone. It made her curious what Elise possibly found sweet about the two. Still, she had to make a stand and not be the baker that allowed bad checks.

"I'll talk to her. We'll work something out."

Elise mimicked wiping her brow. "Glad that's over. I hate conflict. Maybe you could have her work off her bill at the bakery. Doing dishes or something."

While plenty needed to be done in the bakery, she doubted the mother with dubious math skills would go along with such a plan. The last thing she needed was someone unable to do simple business math working the counter.

# CHAPTER FIVE

**B**OTH ELISE AND Della leaned against the dining room wall. The debris of a child's party complete with empty pizza boxes and the remaining back leg and tail of the cupcake dinosaur cake surrounded them. The chocolate icing tempted Della. Sugary foods somehow softened bad news. However, eating her own creation at a party wouldn't go over well, even if the customer hadn't paid for it.

The information about the NSF check for her current clown appearance annoyed Della. Vendors trod a thin line of protecting themselves and not offending the possible buying public. Sure, one individual might end up stiffing them with reasons ranging from bad accounting to a payment not posted in a timely fashion. Dealing with the situation in a delicate fashion could result in several word-of-mouth referrals. Treating the individual or company that mismanaged their funds as a criminal usually resulted in an antagonistic relationship and generally a slow or no payment.

Some vendors turned the non-payers over to collection agencies who had all the personalities of leeches. As a face-to-face business, Della couldn't resort to such a measure. Instead, she'd have to pull up her snake lizard leggings and talk to her customer after most of the children left. Otherwise, the woman wouldn't stand a chance of even hearing her.

Elise shifted weight from foot to foot, demonstrating her unease at being the messenger of bad news.

"Go on, Elise. You've done your part. I suspect we'll head out in about thirty minutes. In fact, you could leave now since there's minimal clean-up to do. No dishes to collect or tables to bus."

The high school student's face brightened. "Oh, could I? Hate to leave you in the lurch, but my morning started early with the SAT test. Knowing my college choice depends on my test score sucked most of the energy out of me." Her hand gestured to the stampeding children as they rushed past her.

One freckle-faced boy must have thought the gesture served as a signal. He stopped and squirted her with the flower corsage. That explained where the trick corsage went. All the gags were officially accounted for. Before Elise could say another word, Della gave a simple wave of her glove-clad hand, dismissing her from the area. At least one person should be able to escape from this disaster.

Not feeling the desire to entertain at the most recent news, Della pulled out a dining room chair and sat. She rested her face on one gloved hand aware of the possibility of rubbing off makeup, but not caring. Baking cookies, creating breath-taking cakes, and catering delicious meals played major roles in her career fantasy. Dealing with bad checks, rowdy children, or dressing up as a clown hardly entered into it. Professions are never what you think they are. Her friend, Lorna, who attended high school with her, always wanted to be a writer. Even though she'd experienced some success with her first two books, the marketing and promotion overwhelmed her. For every dollar she made, she spent two in advertising. Thankfully, she still had her day job, but maybe she gave that up since she'd had a recent signing at Bookmania. Only celebrities showed up for signings.

Another child, a girl with a serious expression and thick glasses, approached. Unsure if she'd be assaulted by another gag, Della jerked upright. At this point, only the bag of laughs should remain. Every now and then, she heard its mechanical laughter echoing down the hall, reminiscent of a county fair funhouse.

The girl cocked her head, giving Della a thorough survey. Finally, she pushed her slipping glasses up and announced, "I've heard clowns are really sad."

"I've heard that, too." Normally, a small child's opinion mattered little to her, but for some reason she didn't want to be viewed as a sad clown. "I'm not a full-time clown."

The somber-faced girl nodded, but then said, "You're still sad."

The little girl was perceptive. "That, I am."

The child placed a hand over hers and for the briefest moment, Della expected to be buzzed. Nothing happened except for a shared moment of solitude. Finally, the girl sighed. "I get it. I'm sad, too. I didn't want to come. My mother made me. She told me it would be good to be around kids my age." She blew out a long breath. "I'm around them all week. Weekends are supposed to be breaks. Why can't I have a break?"

It was a good question and not one Della could answer. In the background, the shrieking ended, and she could hear adult voices and doors closing which meant the party ended with the arrival of the parents. It was none too soon. The small hand over hers made her remember what it felt like being a square peg in a round-hole world. "Have you tried to explain this to your mother?"

"Yes." She withdrew her hand, crossed her arms, and frowned, possibly disappointed with the sad clown answer. Her nose wrinkled. "Dropping me off here served more as a time off for her. She probably went and did something fun."

Parents needed downtime, too. Children might not understand that, so Della searched her memory for things she'd liked to do at that age. "You like to read?"

"All the time," the girl replied, her face joyful. "I'd rather be reading at home than here." Her brows knitted together, and her mouth formed an O. "I mean not at the party, not talking to you."

How sweet. She was trying not to hurt the feelings of the sad clown. "No worries. Did you know there are book clubs at the library, science workshops at the science center, and you can even volunteer to work at the zoo, but you need to be a bit older for that. Find something you'd like to do." She held up her index finger that appeared bigger and more eye-catching in its gloved form. "You'll need to find a club or activity before you suggest it to your mother. In my experience, you're the one who's interested, which means *you* have to do the research. Otherwise, you'll end up at parties like these."

A tall, slender woman with slicked back hair in a low bun entered the room and halted briefly as if expecting applause or admiration. "Emmeline, there you are. I was worried when you weren't with the other children." She directed a suspicious glare at Della, who felt compelled to reply.

"We were talking about the science programs available for kids her age. A love of reading and science starts young."

The disapproving brow smoothed into a more thoughtful one as she turned to her daughter. "Would you like that, pumpkin?"

The formerly solemn Emmeline clapped her hands and twirled with delight. "Yes, I would!" She turned to give Della a thumbs up before dashing after her parent.

Well, at least one of them had abandoned her sad mood. Maybe her mother might wander in and suggest a robotic workshop or growing crystals, although today, it might take something more.

Finally, the bad check writer stumbled into the room and started stacking discarded pizza boxes. She stopped when she saw Della. "Oh!" She started, dropping one of the boxes. "I didn't know you were still here."

"Yeah, I am." Della searched for the right way to start an awkward conversation. Nothing. "Ah, there's something we need to discuss."

The tired mother continued to collect empty pizza boxes but stopped long enough for her lips to form a weak smile. "I know. The kids were out of control. I thought so, too. Didn't expect that many to arrive. Usually, you get about sixty percent who accept. *Everyone* accepted, and a few brought siblings." She shook her head. "I wasn't expecting that."

Anyone other than Della, with eyes and a kind heart, would sense the woman's fragile state and probably decide to say nothing. Those folks probably had a lot more money in the bank. Besides, Della's toes still ached from the foot-stomping her yellow boots endured under persistent, childish feet. In a couple of years, the stomper's mother would have to drive to outlet malls to find shoes big enough.

Maybe the best she could do was treat it like a bandage. "Your check bounced."

The expression on the tired mama's face froze into place, and her eyelashes fluttered as she replied. "That's impossible."

Denial. One of the possibilities she expected. If Mabel knew, it meant she'd been going through the bakery bank account or received an email from the bank. Since her mother had lent her money for the bakery and cosigned for it, both their names were on the account.

Della's fingers dipped into the pocket of her gingham dress and retrieved her phone. It took about a minute and a half of scrolling to find the bank email. She opened it, then passed the phone to the indignant woman.

"Oh my! I'm not sure how this happened. Give me a minute. I need to check my bank account." She left the room just as Mabel entered with a check in her hand.

"Sweetie, I wanted to let you know Grandma wrote me a check for everything. No need to say anything."

"Now you tell me." Della grimaced, thinking about the last uncomfortable minutes. "I'm almost done here if you want to wait in the car. I'll even let you play with the radio."

This made them both chuckle since it had been a bribe her mother used to use on a much younger Della. Mabel stacked a few boxes and scraped the trash into one corner of the table before leaving. It probably killed her not to be able to clear the table completely.

The front door closed in the distance. Della turned, surprised to see her customer in question trembling and white-faced. "All my money is gone. There's nothing. My check just got deposited on Thursday. Now there's nothing. I don't know what to tell you."

In the face of such a devastating shock, cupcakes and clowns were the least of her troubles. Della stood, ready to depart. "Don't worry about it. I'm sure there's a number you can call and work it out. Got to go." She waved, hoping her mother had gathered up any remaining supplies since she had no intention of intruding on the woman anymore.

As she headed out of the room, she heard the woman mutter to herself, "At least my nit-picking mother-in-law doesn't know."

# CHAPTER SIX

ARDENED SNOW CRUNCHED under Della's yellow rainboots as
she made her way to her mother's car. Since they hadn't
catered the party, the large sedan had served to carry the cupcakes
creation, what they did need, and themselves. Thank goodness for
that. The cost of renting a van would be money she wasn't getting
back. The frigid wind pushing against her billowy dress hurried her
step, resulting in an unexpected slide and fall on the slick driveway.
Stunned by her feet moving forward when her body chose to go the
other direction, Della stared up at the sky, noticing the lack of
clouds.

A car door slammed. "Della! Are you all right?"

Afraid her mother might slip on the icy patch, she pushed up
into a sitting position and held up a hand to stop her. "I'm okay.
Watch your step. It's slippery."

"I know that! It's not my first winter in the Midwest, you know.
I've got some decent tread on my boots. Decent shoes are what you
need." Her mother stopped, realizing the reason behind the
impractical boots. "Spring will be here before you know it. I can
smell it in the air."

Exhaust from the fleet of departed cars that had arrived to pick
up their precious darlings lingered in the air. Not exactly spring in
her opinion. Her mother, always the optimist, tried to put a better

face on things.

Della decided to play along. She pushed into a crouched position, debating if it would be safer to duck-walk down the drive than standing. At least she wouldn't have as far to fall. Dignity won out as she stood.

"You're right, Mom. Spring *is* on its way."

A loud crack sounded. Della reacted, turning fast in the direction of the sound in time to witness an ice-laden tree branch hitting the ground, sending out a flurry of snow. Too bad nature hadn't received the memo about better weather, even if it was wishful thinking. That groundhog shadow thing must apply to states more southern than her own. No matter if the groundhog saw or didn't see its shadow, they still had six and sometimes *more* weeks of winter. Keeping a wary eye on the tree, she made her way to the car and slid into the passenger seat.

Even though she preferred to drive, the boots and the outfit might not function in a wreck or a possible traffic stop. People never took a clown seriously. Who caused the wreck? Had to be the clown. A rolling stop or a tad over the speed limit would snag a ticket. Even though women swore crying got them out of a ticket, a crying clown would be ugly, and messy, and possibly considered an act.

"I'm ready to get out of here. That driveway is a skating rink. I don't remember it being that bad on arrival."

"It wasn't. The weather warmed up, things melted, and then the temperature dropped, freezing everything again." The car keys jingled as she twisted them into the ignition. The car purred to life with the vents blasting warm air. Steel band music floated out of the speakers—something about a yellow bird. Even though her mood veered far from upbeat, she knew better than to complain. Her mother would say driver picks the music. When a passenger, she'd point out good manners meant the passenger chose the tunes. In the end, her mother controlled the radio if in the car.

Della asked, "Spring music?"

"Happy tunes. We all have to do what we can to survive winter."

"So true. I wish I could have sold the council on Mardi Gras, but realistically, that stuff takes time. I need to start meeting other business owners and bring up the subject. It has to be better than being a clown. No wonder we have no clowns in town."

"It was just one party."

"Yeah, but it was a doozy. Yes, I know I have four more to go. Let's hope they're better. I did meet an interesting girl who hated being there. Reminded me a little of myself. Here I am, having a decent exchange with her, when her mother arrives and shoots me a look that screams creepy clown. When I tried to tell her we were talking about her daughter being part of the science workshop down at the center, the woman froze me out."

"No surprise there." Her mother shifted into drive and pulled the car hard to the left to execute a U-turn to leave the neighborhood. "Kathy, the daughter of the grandmother, pointed out a woman that may have been. She called her an out-of-towner who thinks she's all that. She knew her from work. Besides, no one wants advice on child-rearing from a childless clown."

"How could she know I was childless?"

"You're doing children's parties where every other mother is running errands or chauffeuring their child to various events."

"Good point, but it doesn't preclude me from having children."

The car stopped at the end of the neighborhood as a steady stream of traffic made them wait. With Owens' increased population, getting out could take forever. Her mother must have spied an opening. She stomped on the gas and fishtailed before gaining the lane.

Della closed her eyes and grabbed the door handle for dear life as the car tires slid across the slick payment and then jerked as they found traction. Her mother took that as a sign to goose the gas again, causing the car to leapfrog forward.

No one appreciated backseat or passenger seat drivers, but Della hoped to live a little longer. Perhaps a conversation might keep her mother from behaving as if she were in some auto rally. "What's your take on the mother-in-law?"

"She thinks her son married beneath him, but most mothers do."

This tidbit earned a smidgen of sympathy for bad-check woman. It couldn't be easy knowing whatever she did, her mother-in-law was second-guessing her. "You think Grandma is good for it?"

"I'd bet my match-making reputation on it."

Della cleared her throat. "You don't have a matchmaking reputation."

"I would if you'd cooperate. What about Todd and Eileen?"

The names sounded vaguely familiar. Maybe they were one of the couples her parents invited over for cookouts. "Were they the ones with the toy poodle they always brought or were they the yellers?"

"Ah, the yellers. Okay, maybe not the best pairing, but they did have the same communication style, which is a plus. Anyhow, back to Grandma. I know her in the way I know most folks in town. I recognize the face and name. Once I started talking to her, I remembered her from the women's group, The Miracle Whips. Before you ask, it originated due to the love of making mayonnaise-based salads."

"That's a thing they had to have a group for?"

Mabel sniffed and swerved into the other lane without signaling. "Don't act so high and mighty with me. I happen to know you were part of a cartoon fan club."

"I was a kid."

"You were fifteen."

Geesh! A person had no secrets around her mother. Maybe she should have been on the force. With her around, the rest of the police could take a well-earned coffee break. "Back to the woman who is paying for the party."

A honk sounded nearby. An angry honk in Della's opinion, but her mother ignored it, as she did most unpleasant things. Even though it would irritate her mother, she leaned over enough to see the speedometer, which was over fifty and approaching sixty. "Road's slick."

"I know. Anyhow, I was telling you about Ethel."

"Who?"

"Grandma with the checkbook."

"Oh, yeah. I'm surprised people still write checks. I heard on a radio show about identity fraud that all the information you need to create a false account or apply for a credit card is on most checks."

"Maybe. All the same, Ethel likes to be seen as Lady Bountiful, the big shot. It probably thrilled her she could pay for the party. She'll make sure to mention it to her son and a few other folks. No way would she write you a bad check. It wouldn't fit with her image."

It wouldn't make sense, either, for someone who valued personal image to be sloppy with their checking account. Della heaved a sigh of relief and sunk back into the car's plush upholstery until she spotted the roundabout sign. City planners decided Owens needed roundabouts instead of four-way stops and built as many as they could afford. Problems resulted when people often turned the wrong way into the roundabout or didn't slow down enough to navigate the circle. "Mom! The roundabout."

"What?" Mabel glanced at her daughter but thankfully slowed down as they entered the roundabout. Her mother handled the big car adeptly, covering almost eighty percent of the circle without incident. To think Della had worried.

*Boom!*

The car lurched forward, sliding to a stop as Mabel stomped on the brakes, forcing the seatbelt harnesses to tighten in place as they flew toward the dashboard only to be stopped from making contact by a hard snap.

Mabel gasped, "I think someone hit us!"

Having been warned against saying *what can happen next*, Della sucked in her lips, trapping the words inside. On the plus side, her mother wasn't the culprit, and Della, in her clown attire, wasn't behind the wheel.

# Chapter Seven

T HE MEAGER WINTER sun set low on the horizon, reminding everyone to hurry home before the final drop. Winter nights blanketed the city with an inky blackness that managed to feel both endless and malevolent. The leafless trees stretched out their branches as if survivors of a natural disaster signaling for help.

Despite the many times Della suffered through winter in the Midwest, it felt like a marathon to make it to spring—not that she ever ran a marathon, but it must feel something like this. The fender bender from behind must be something like a marathoner stumbling close to the finish line.

When hit from behind, most people would yelp or curse. A few would do both. One or two might even spring from their cars, threatening a lawsuit or grabbing the back of their neck, screaming, "Whiplash!"

Not Mabel Delacroix. She peered into her rear-view mirror. "Oh my! It's the woman from the lingerie department at The White House department store. Mrs. Cooper. I thought she retired. Maybe I didn't see her the last few times I updated my foundation collection."

Those not involved in the crash either honked or worked their way around the stalled cars with their driver's side tires riding the curb, tilting their vehicles at an awkward angle. It was not smart at all and could possibly cause another accident. Others made a U-turn to seek out another route to get to where they needed to be.

"Mrs. Cooper or not," Della prompted, "we need to call the police and exchange insurance information. I'm certain both cars are drivable."

With her eyes still on the mirror, Mabel replied as her brows knitted together. "Oh my, she looks worried."

"Not surprising. She did hit you. Her insurance rates will go up." A quick glance over her shoulder revealed a white-haired senior gripping the wheel with a tiny dog wearing a hairbow with its paws on the steering wheel. That would so not go over well when the officer arrived. A wave of compassion swept over her, thinking how upset the poor dear must be.

"I could go talk to her."

"Would you?" Mabel's expression brightened as she put the car in park and switched on her emergency lights. "I'll just call the police. Not sure I can face someone I bought shapewear from."

Her mother's explanation made no sense. "Do you think she'll remember you and start blabbing your purchases all over town?"

"No!" Mabel pressed both hands to her chest. "That would be terrible. Not sure why she would. She hit *me*, not the other way around."

The click of the door lock releasing sounded before Della swung her door open. Occasionally, she'd been accused of not being able to take a joke, which must be a family trait. "Joke. It was a joke. A good portion of the women in town buy shapewear. Not sure why it's a big deal."

Mabel sniffed and shot her one of those long-suffering looks mothers somehow perfected between the months of knowing they're pregnant and giving birth. It could be used on multiple occasions and for different purposes. When Della complained about her play costume not being exactly like the other girls' costumes, she got the look. No one had bothered to explain everything the expression meant, but it wouldn't be out of place for someone to sing in the background in a gravelly bass about the troubles they'd seen.

Her mother heaved a sigh before adding, "Suspecting someone is wearing the latex equivalent of a steel drum is not the same as knowing. Go assure Mrs. Cooper everything is okay, and help is on the way."

Della gave her mother a thumbs up before closing the door. Her yellow rainboots squeaked and slid in the slush, making the experience a little unnerving. Each step held the promise of a slide or pitching backward. A car coming from a perpendicular street slowed and a window lowered. The sound had Della turning expectantly to what could be a generous offer to help.

An apple-cheeked kid stuck his head out the window and hooted, "Clowns can't drive!"

The window slid up quickly, most likely closed by the driver. Just as well. Della might have found herself defending her driving skills to a child. *Must focus on the task on hand*, she reminded herself as her gaze moved to the bumper that rested close to her mother's bumper. There was definite crumpling plus missing paint. All the same, it was minimal damage that would probably cost around three thousand dollars to fix. If a car could be made into a jigsaw puzzle and the part that needed to be fixed could be exchanged for a new piece, shouldn't the new piece be in relationship to the total cost of the car? If so, her mother owned an expensive vehicle. At one time, the sticker price may have scared off a few folks, but her father wanted his wife to have a nice car with all the bells and whistles. Since her dad had bought the car, her mother would drive it until the wheels dropped off.

Fortunately, the wheels stayed on. As Della drew closer to the other car, another furry face popped up complete with curious eyes, an adorable button nose, and a barrette securing its canine topknot. *Two little distractions* are what her father would label them. Della waved with her gloved hand and was about to tap on the window when it went down.

"Good heavens! A clown. What else can go wrong?"

Apparently, no one told her the dangers of uttering the last sentence. So much for the fearful old lady. She sounded testy. "Ah, hello. I was in the car in front. The one you hit."

"Yeah, yeah, I know what happened. It was the weather. An act of God, you can't fault a person for that. Any damage to my car?"

"Depends on what you consider damage." Della took a step back, assuming the woman might want to view her own car. She had never encountered Mrs. Cooper before. She would have remembered the acerbic female, but to be fair, it wasn't the best day of the woman's life. Any other day, she might be a sweet senior with a demure smile and a nice compliment for everyone.

The heavy car door creaked open, and one of the adorable twosome jumped out. "Oh no! Terminator!" She turned panicky eyes toward Della. "You have to catch my Terminator!"

Without giving it too much thought, Della jogged in the direction the tiny dog took. If nothing else, it showed sense heading to the side of the road as opposed to into traffic. Dry, brown grasses and stalks clumped together rising about a meter above the crusty snow provided an excellent hiding place for the wee canine. The wind's icy fingers teased the back of her neck and pulled at her fake pigtails. Della chafed her arms as she waded into the deep ditch that must contain the runaway pup. As small as it was, it would need a ladder to climb out. A scratching sound came from an abandoned box stuck in the wintry mire. "Aha! Got you, Terminator."

With any luck, she could carry the runaway back in the box. She flipped open one flap to make sure the box had an intact bottom before she picked it up and allowed the dog to escape again.

"Eek!"

Della stumbled backward, almost sitting, but caught herself before her rear touched the icy ground. A furry face peeped over the edge of the box, but not a cute one. With a single lurch, a possum exited the box and lumbered down the road. On the upside, she hadn't picked up the box. Mrs. Cooper wanted to know what else could go wrong. Returning a possum as opposed to a much-loved Yorkie might rank right up there.

She should have guessed it wouldn't be that easy. Headlights shone in the distance, reminding her of the upcoming night. There was no way she could find the dog in the dark. She wasn't really sure she could find it, period. Why would a spoiled pup come to a stranger, especially one dressed as a clown? Still, she had to try.

"Here, Terminator! Come here." She made kissy sounds and tried to think what might sound good to a cold, lost dog. "How about a nice steak dinner with a sweet potato dripping with butter."

That made her stomach rumble. A whimper sounded to her left. Della headed in the direction of the sound and then stopped. Was it a dog whimper or a possum whimper? What sounds did possums make?

The whimper came again, along with the wind. Della gave an all-over shiver. If she stayed here debating what to do, she'd freeze to death. Perhaps, because she was trying to do a good deed, she wouldn't be rewarded with rabies from a rabid animal bite. With her cold hands stiffening under the lightweight cotton gloves, she might not even feel the bite.

Whining came from beneath a stack of broken branches that served as a type of filter for litterers. Discarded coffee cups, chip bags, and a wadded bag from a local fast-food restaurant decorated the branches.

Della knelt in the snow-filled ditch, not wanting to consider what rested under the patchy cover. She gentled her voice. "Who's momma's little Terminator?"

The whimper increased in volume and urgency. It must be a dog, she assured herself. "C'mon, Termy!" she called, although the dog might not have a nickname. "You can do it, Terminator. Come on out and I'll take you back to your mother."

Nothing. It was probably scared so she tried again, calling the dog everything from *precious* to *darling*. No luck. It might be trapped. This meant—Della gave a heavy sigh—she'd have to pick through the trash pile until she got to the dog. On the upside, she did have gloves. *Thin* gloves. She picked up the coffee cups and tossed them aside as she worked her way through the pile, wondering how people could throw out garbage assuming it magically vanishes.

A minute or so later she reached Terminator, who was held tight by a branch next to a chili cup. Even though the dog squirmed to reach the cup, the branch that held the tiny pup did it a favor. Rancid or not, the chili wouldn't have benefited the Yorkie. Della scooted closer to the dog that broke into frenzied yelping. That's gratitude for you.

She snugged her fingers into Terminator's collar before breaking the branch to release him. The shivering canine provided a scrap of warmth as she pulled it close. All the squatting made standing difficult, and with the help of a nearby sapling, she pulled herself up while she kept a tight hold on Terminator. The flashing lights of the newly arrived police car guided her back where she turned over the complaining dog to its owner.

The woman smiled at Della as she hugged the dog. "I don't know what I'd do without my little Terminator."

The officer at the scene raised one eyebrow at the name but said nothing. Across the road, a large sedan decorated with a half-dozen antennas, which signaled emergency vehicle, storm chaser, or ham radio enthusiast, pulled to a stop and a bulky man exited. He headed their way.

Mrs. Cooper cooed to her lost dog. "It's been a day and a half. I was on my way to pick up treats for the kiddos when I got a call that my credit card on file wasn't working."

"Using a phone while driving?" the officer inquired with a neutral expression.

"Oh, no, Officer. I wouldn't do that." Mrs. Cooper probably realized she'd put her foot in it. "I got a message, an email. I was hurrying to the store to see what was wrong."

Unbelievable. The officer said nothing, probably assuming the woman had been through enough. The officer took photos of the cars and the road, although skid marks would be hard to see in the limited light. Mrs. Cooper stuck to her weather excuse as Della sprinted, the best she could with frozen knees, to her mother's warm car where the silhouette of the husky stranger lingered.

# CHAPTER EIGHT

NXIOUS TO GET back into her mother's warm car, Della
scampered to the passenger side while wondering about who
was engaging her mother in conversation. Who would stop by for a
chat when they saw an obvious accident? A lawyer? It was probably
an ambulance chaser sort, which would explain the antennas on the
car. Did the man cruise the city hoping to find a possible client?

Her mother's voice sounded cheery. Then again, the only thing
that had upset her mother about the wreck was the possibility that
her purchase of shapewear might get out. Della's hand flattened over
the car handle when the man straightened, exposing an older,
grizzled face with bushy brows and a chin line going jowly with age.
"Move along. Nothing to see here."

"And who are you?" Della inquired with a bit of an edge to her
voice as she opened the car door. Would this day never end? It was
so typical of her mother, treating everyone with civility. There had to
be a line drawn somewhere.

"Edward Jennings, Police Commissioner."

Police commissioner? Owens had a police commissioner? That
was a surprise. Della glanced over at her mother as she slipped into
the car. Her mother nodded as if to confirm the man's words. Many
of her father's beliefs remained with Della, and one of them was
titles were unimportant. What matters was a person's actions. Too

tired, too cold, and not impressed that the commissioner showed up at their accident, all the same, civility demanded a reply. "Della Delacroix, baker, caterer, and sometime clown."

"I noticed the last part," he nodded his head and smirked.

A real laugh riot. Della tried for a smile but didn't feel it happening. "Birthday party."

Her mother added, "We're both tired from it. The kids have so much energy."

"I hear you," the commissioner acknowledged. "Let's see if I can speed things up and get you two lovely ladies home."

Her mother giggled at the heavy-handed compliment and put up the window as the commissioner moved away.

Della rolled her eyes. "Where was he when we needed help with the catnappers a few months ago?"

Her mother's shoulders went up in a shrug. "No clue. He seems nice."

"He's patronizing."

Her mother *tsked* and reached over the console to pat her hand. "Hungry? You sound hungry. You always get grumpy when you have to wait to eat."

Not always, only sometimes. "You'd think the hostess would have offered us a piece of pizza. I didn't even get a drink. Yes, I'm hungry, thirsty, cold, and finding it hard to be civil."

"I know, sweetie. It's showing."

"*You* were able to hide with the mother and sister-in-law."

"Outside in the cold," Mabel made sure to point out.

"True, but you chose it over being in a heated house with wild second graders. What does that say?"

Her mother chuckled. "You got me. The cold I could bear. We

took turns sitting in each other's cars, too. Tell you what, I'll handle anything else that needs to be done with the accident. You stay in the car and get warm. Oh, look." Mabel glanced into a rearview mirror. "Here comes the officer with the commissioner. I should get out. Hand me my wallet."

Della reached into her mother's tote bag, withdrew the wallet, and handed it to her. Mabel checked the emergency brake before exiting the car.

To defrost her frozen limbs, Della jacked up the heat. The noisy heater fan blocked out any conversation, but Della kept an eye on the rearview mirror. The headlights from both Mrs. Cooper's car and the police car illuminated the scene. Mrs. Cooper, with her furry distractions, stayed in the car while the officer, commissioner, and her mother huddled close by. A slash of white exchanged hands, possibly the accident report. Her mother's posture suddenly stiffened. She pivoted and marched the few steps back to the car. Had they charged her with the accident? Della shook her head at the nonsensical possibility.

Mabel opened the door, handed the report to Della, took her seat, and fastened her safety belt with aggressive movements. "We can leave now." She released the brake and put the car into drive. Away from the helpful headlights, Della squinted at the report to no effect. "How did they justify blaming you for the accident?"

Her mother snorted. "They didn't."

"That's good, right?" It sure didn't explain her mother's odd behavior. To be fair, she gave up a Saturday for this. Certainly, better options existed than accompanying her daughter to children's birthday parties. Guilt tugged at her. "I'm sorry. I really shouldn't have asked you to help with the party. I imagine you could have met a friend for lunch. Anything would have been better."

Her mother's long sigh filled the car. "It's not that. I was glad to go. I had a decent chat during the party." She shook her head. "The party, while not fun, didn't bother me. That *woman*,"—she snarled the word—"made a point of mentioning to the officer and commissioner that she knew me as a customer from the foundation department. There was no reason to do that. Tacky. That's what it was."

"I agree. However, most men don't understand what foundation garments are. If Mrs. Cooper meant to embarrass you, it would have been a fail."

"Oh, really?" Her mother's voice brightened. "All the same, she should have been charged with the accident."

Della's brow furrowed as she put together the information. "You weren't charged. Mrs. Cooper wasn't charged. Then, who was?"

"Apparently, the weather," her mother offered in a derisive manner.

"I believe that was Mrs. Cooper's plan all along. Still, I feel sorry for her—a little. She mentioned she was on the phone and found out she couldn't buy her gourmet dog treats. Not sure what happened, but I thought maybe her credit wasn't good. There seems to be a lot of that happening around here, including Clarice, then our client, now Mrs. Cooper. It's almost a thing."

"You know..." Her mother spoke as she maneuvered through the almost empty streets. "...I saw a show about how all these people were ripped off by someone stealing their identities."

That would not be good, and the very last thing Della needed. Mounting anxiety forced her to inquire. "Was this show based on an actual event or fiction?"

Her mother remained silent as they pulled into Della's apartment complex. Not stellar in the summer with its color faded siding, the block of locked mailboxes leaned slightly, possibly held in place by the ice. The lack of landscaping showed even more in the winter, giving the place a slightly abandoned appearance. Only the cars parked in front of the buildings announced otherwise.

Finally, her mother spoke as she parked beside Della's aging compact. "I can't remember if it was fiction or real. Even the shows based on real crimes hire actors to enact the crime. On the other hand, crime show dramas are often based on the headlines. It's six of the one and a half dozen of the other."

Ready to shower, eat, and don some sweats, Della reached into the back for her bag. "How did the con people get so much information on the victims?"

"I think it was investment or insurance. Something where they asked for your bank information. No one suspected anything until their account was emptied out."

There was no need for Della to worry since she had no money to invest. "I appreciate your helping out."

"No problem. It wasn't a total waste."

"How so?" Della had her hand on the door handle and depressed it, letting in a strip of cold air as she waited for her mother's answer. Bad party. Bad check. Car wreck. It sounded like a waste of a day to her.

Her mother giggled, suddenly acting coy. "Edward asked for my number, so he could check on me."

"Edward?" No silver-haired gentleman had shown up at the party. If so, he hadn't come in and why would he want to check on her mother? Most men would simply mention going for a cup of coffee.

"Oh, you know, the commissioner."

Her mother acted as if Della should have caught the reference. She must mean Mr. Big Shot. Della wasn't impressed, not impressed at all, but she knew enough not to say so. "When did this happen?"

"When we were exchanging information. Edward told me he was concerned about my health and would like to follow up with a call to make sure no medical issues came up. That's when Mrs. Cooper had to announce I was a frequent shopper in the foundation department."

"Did you give him your number?" It sounded a bit like a legitimate police procedure, but she wouldn't swear to it having never been in a wreck. Her mother acted as if it were a prelude to a date.

Her mother's jaw dropped. "Oh no! I stomped off angry that Mrs. Cooper made me sound like a frequent foundation shopper. I must have forgotten." Both her hands framed her face, and she growled.

Talk about unexpected behavior. "Mother, are you okay?"

Her hands dropped, she took a deep breath, and then answered. "I'm angry. That's what I am. No reason for the foundation remark, except to embarrass me. Just mean. She only did that to make me look bad in front of Edward."

Mere steps away her apartment waited, complete with a hot shower and food in the fridge. Della needed to wind up the conversation. "Your phone number should be on the police record. If he wants to call you, he can."

With that, she left a beaming mother and hurried up the stairs, only to have her phone start ringing with a number that hadn't come across her phone in an exceptionally long time. Thank goodness for caller ID.

# CHAPTER NINE

ELLA'S PHONE CHIMED again as she stepped onto the stairs leading up to her apartment. The phone lit up, displaying the name of her friend, Lorna, whom she hadn't talked to in ages. After school, they'd drifted apart. There were no big fights or misunderstandings over a boy. Instead, they had pursued different interests. Baking exerted its pull on Della while writing remained Lorna's focus, but about six months ago, maybe more, Della accidentally attended Lorna's book signing at the local Bookmania shop.

The newest release by a world-famous baker had brought Della to the store. Noise from the setup for the signing intrigued her and had her peeking out of the cooking section. When she recognized Lorna, her attempt to say *hello* ended with a grim-looking staff member demanding to see her ticket. Apparently, attendees of the book signing had to pre-purchase their ticket along with an expensive hardback version of Lorna's release. So no, she couldn't count that as renewing their friendship.

The phone chiming finally ended, its cessation bringing her back to the present and with it, a sense of relief and guilt. Relief she didn't have to delve into one more thing tonight and guilt for neglecting a friend, even an almost forgotten one.

She sighed and unlocked her door. Della knew she'd call her back if only to satisfy her curiosity. The phone chimed again, and it was Lorna.

"Hello, Lorna. Long time." Della waited, expecting a similar greeting or possibly an invite to the school reunion. Why else would she call?

"Thank goodness I reached you. Is your father still a cop?" she queried in a breathy voice.

"Technically a detective." Even beyond the grave, she felt he had earned his detective title and to not use it would negate his hard work, but why would Lorna call her? If she had any questions about the law, she could go online and look it up.

"Good."

Obviously, Lorna had missed the news that Detective Delacroix had gone to the big squad room in the sky. "Lorna, my father is dead. It's been about seven years now."

"Oh no!"

That sounded a tad ominous. Sure, it could be an *oh no, I just stuck my foot in my mouth,* but it didn't sound that way. There was a little more emotion than that, which meant the exclamation related to something personal.

Della opened her door, dropped her bag in the hallway, and locked the door, all while keeping the phone in place by hunching up her shoulder. She winced as she realized her phone face would be covered with clown makeup.

What could be so difficult about being a successful writer? Did she have a block, a plot hole, or maybe wanted to talk to Della's father about a police procedural matter? "How can I help you?"

A teary gulp sounded and then a sniff. "I'm not sure if you can. Your father struck me as a nice person who'd hear someone out."

"True enough." Della moved toward the fridge for a much-needed drink, but her hand stilled on the door as she considered the words. Something had happened and urgent from the sound of it. "I'm pretty fair and impartial. Maybe I could help. I've assisted in solving a couple of local crimes recently."

"Oh…" A note of hopefulness blossomed in her voice. "You're a cop, too?"

"No, a baker."

There was silence at the other end of the line, which could mean a dropped call. "Lorna?"

"I'm here at the hospital and was hoping for someone who would believe me."

"Tell me." Della swung open the fridge, grabbed a chilled bottle of water, shut the door, and took a seat on her sofa to listen to what she intuited might be a long, convoluted tale.

"Out of the blue, two guys break into my house. I'm home, and I think it must be a mistake. Who breaks into a condo that's occupied?"

"Did you call the police?" Most people would have at the first suspicious sound. Her father enjoyed relating calls involving late-arriving teens or even raccoons setting off the burglar alarm.

"I wanted to, but I had plugged my phone into the charger in the living room. I was in my office reading my email. I ran for the back door, assuming they didn't want me, but whatever they could steal. One of them caught me fleeing, and I reached for the first thing on the kitchen counter as he tackled me."

"Coffee pot?" Della guessed. Many an evildoer had been surprised by a hot pot of coffee thrown at them. It was odd your mouth could accept steaming liquid, but not the rest of your body.

"No, it was my skillet. Unfortunately, I didn't make as much contact as I'd like. He had a short crowbar and used it until I was unconscious. Before I blacked out, I saw the other guy with my laptop. He said something about how they'd be the famous author now and be millionaires. Stupid animals!"

"That's horrible! You called the police, right?" The last thing their sleepy little town needed was two thugs like that. They must be from out of town. Surely Della and her mother had helped lock up any local baddies. Della perched on the edge of the sofa cushion as she listened.

"I called 911. Told them I'd been attacked. The ambulance came first. The EMT thought I had a concussion. Also, a cut on my arm that took stitches. Three good-sized bumps on the head and a fractured clavicle. I ended up using the skillet as a shield. The EMT said it may have saved my life. Good chance the fools thought they killed me. No sense at all. Do they think being a writer is simply stealing a computer?" She growled a few other words that probably weren't meant to be heard.

"Did you tell the police this?"

"I did. They sent this one detective who acted like he didn't want to waste time talking to me. Once he heard I was an author, he asked me if this was a publicity stunt. A publicity stunt!"

She could understand why Lorna called. When their last case needed police assistance, Della and her mother had run into a detective who'd transferred in from the big city who referred to her as Nancy Drew, Girl Detective. He believed nothing happened in the small town of Owens and acted accordingly.

"So, not cool. Maybe I can do something from my end. I'm sure a forensic team will have been dispatched to your house." There was no need to mention the team would have to send everything off elsewhere to be analyzed, which would take time.

"You're right. No way I'd have my door ripped off as a publicity stunt since I'll be paying for it myself." Her sigh carried heavily over the phone. "The doctor gave me a sedative or something to deal with the shock. All the same, they're watching me, I think, for signs of internal bleeding or swelling of the brain due to blunt force trauma. I may not even be making any sense."

"So far, you're making sense. I'm still baffled by the criminals who stole your computer. How do they think that will make them into you, a rich and famous writer?"

Coughing sounded in Della's ear. Finally, it resolved into a harsh chuckle. "Me? Famous? Me? Rich? If Stupid and Stupider had any sense, they'd realize a wealthy writer wouldn't be living in Owens' retirement community. Thank goodness my neighbor agreed to keep an eye on my place while I'm gone. Another neighbor volunteered to cover the broken doorway with plywood. Everyone loved my grandmother. I guess I inherited the love along with her place."

Owens' small size merited only one retirement community, Silver Hills. People joked that the *Silver* in the name referred to the residents' hair color. The basic ranch condos usually shared a driveway. A landscaping company performed all snow removal and lawn services. Her mother joked about moving there but abandoned the notion immediately because it would make her feel old to be a resident. Never mind the fact most of her neighbors were senior citizens. From what she could remember from a bike ride through the place, none of the units rated the term *luxurious*. They were clean and well-kept but far from golf course community lavish.

Della's weary mind wrestled with what to do next. The thieves probably assumed they had all of Lorna's work on the computer.

Somehow, they'd start copyrighting everything and assume the rights. A while back a rather well-known author had taken in a handsome drifter, who wormed his way into her affections. Before the family knew what happened, all the books' copyrights were in his name, which the family discovered after her death. Who knew what it took for that to happen? Right now, the culprits might assume they'd kill Lorna and possibly lie low, or they could be busy changing everything to their names.

"Did you call anyone, like your editor or publisher?"

A moan sounded at the other end. "It hurts to think. Don't know what I did. I think I called my agent, Liz."

"That's good. It's a start. Do you have anything publishable on the laptop? A finished book, perhaps?"

"No, not really. I was playing with a story with a friend. Her email was what I was reading when they broke in. I'm sure you've heard of authors daring each other to write specific stories or particular genres?"

She hadn't. "Go on."

"Silly. We were writing as if for the Bulwer-Lytton Fiction Contest."

Lorna said it in such a casual fashion that Della thought she should know what it was but didn't. Too tired to pretend, she asked, "Bulward what?"

"Bulwer-Lytton Fiction Contest. It's a contest started a decade ago by some professors at a California college. I don't know the whole back story. The contest was for the worst written start of a story. Well, we were writing paragraphs to each other. I'd write one atrocious paragraph and then she'd add on to the story with one even worse. We kept emailing the story to each other. That's all I had on that computer. My original laptop had a meltdown about five days ago. The computer they took was a cheapie I bought at the discount mart until the replacement one arrives."

Still puzzled by the idea of writers penning bad lines, Della asked, "Why would you write bad paragraphs to each other?"

"To blow off steam between books. We spend so much time trying to remember what *not* to do. Sometimes, it's fun to do every bad thing, such as start a sentence with a conjunction and end it with a preposition, not use any punctuation, be extremely wordy, use the wrong modifier, plus interrupt a thought with an aside."

"Okay." Even though she didn't get the fun in such activity, she knew one thing. "We'll need to keep an eye out for your Bulkhard Linton tale."

"Bulwer-Ly—never mind, I forgot what the name was." She moaned. "My jaw hurts, too. The doctor told me I was lucky my jaw wasn't shattered. Did I mention it was horrible writing?"

"You did, but would the miscreants who broke into your house with the intent of stealing your writing identity know it was bad?"

"Probably not."

"It's a starting point, and I might know someone who can run interference for you. I'll let you know tomorrow."

A voice sounded in the distance—something about checking vitals. "I've got to go. The nurse is here."

The phone disconnected, leaving Della staring at it. Something was going on in this town, and it needed to be dealt with before it got out of control, *if* it wasn't already.

# Chapter Ten

A FTER DELLA ENDED her disturbing conversation with Lorna, she stared at her phone, all thoughts of a hot shower and climbing into bed momentarily forgotten. Gunshots and the screech of tire wheels startled her, only to be followed by an equally loud commercial about grabbing mattresses while they were hot. Her neighbors listened to their television much too loud. To be fair, they usually turned it off by ten at night.

The early evening twilight often fooled her into thinking it was later than it was. A peek at her phone reminded her it wasn't even six. It was too early for bed unless she wanted to wake up around three in the morning. Right now, she had to handle the most pressing concerns first.

Della yanked off the awful wig with a yelp due to forgetting about the bobby pins holding it in place. She removed her clown makeup and even managed a shower. By then, her mother should have arrived home.

Should she call her mother? Not only had her mother wasted her Saturday at the birthday party topped off by a fender bender, but her parent might also be waiting for a call from the *I'm So Important Police Commissioner Guy*. The possibility made her grimace. For the last couple of years, she'd been urging her mother to date. Still, she wasn't overly thrilled with the commissioner, but as she pointed out originally, it might be strictly a courtesy call.

If she didn't alert her mother to Lorna's situation, Clarice, being a nurse and privy to all the hospital emergency intakes, would know and share the gossip. Once Della related the story, her mother would get that sad puppy face due to hearing it from Clarice first as opposed to her own daughter. The expression featured a trembling bottom lip and accusing eyes—a judgmental puppy. She'd feel about two inches high. There was no reason for that scenario to happen, especially since she needed her mother's resources to discover needed details.

Mabel Delacroix would tap into her gossip hotline and information would pour in almost as fast as the Internet. The exception would be her mother's tidbits would be more pinpointed to Owens and not created by a marketing algorithm.

After a hastily slapped together sandwich, and with her hair still damp, Della booted up her laptop and searched for *Identity Theft*, giving her mother some time to reconnect with Tony, her rescue pup, before calling.

Red melting letters flowed across her computer screen giving *Identity Theft* about the same treatment as a cheap horror movie title. It could be just as frightening, lasting more than ninety minutes and didn't stop when you stepped out of the theater. The four major types of identity theft included medical, criminal, financial, and child identity. Medical? Della's brows puckered. It was news to her. She continued to read about how people used others' insurance cards to get treatment with the owner's permission about half the time. It seems to be a common event that relatives and sometimes friends would lend their insurance card to uninsured folks. Perhaps they rationalized that since they were paying for insurance, someone should get the benefit of it. No wonder the receptionist at her doctor's office always asked for her identification along with her insurance card.

Criminal identity theft occurred when a stopped person identified him or herself as someone else to avoid being nabbed for an outstanding warrant or to avoid a ticket in their name. A simple traffic stop could turn into an arrest.

Her lips firmed as she remembered her father talking about aliases. Most people tried to stay close to their own names or used a name familiar to themselves. A middle name could serve as a first name while a mother's maiden name worked for a last. She didn't think anyone she'd met today had a criminal using their name with the exception of Lorna.

"The third type…" She read aloud. "…is financial identity theft. Bingo!"

Financial identity theft occurs when a person uses another's personal information to gain goods, information, or services. Most of the people she'd dealt with had complained about money, not services. If any one of her dissatisfied folks had been spies or scientists handling military secrets, then she could see the why behind the identity theft in regards to information. Instead, today's disasters centered around a dwindling bank account or a debit card fail. It made her wonder about the culprit who would have to *not* know his victim to pick someone as memorable and well known as Clarice to try to both emulate and fleece simultaneously.

The fourth type of theft happened to be child identity theft. This usually occurred among people who knew the child and the accompanying social security number. A child is unlikely to have a record, which allowed someone to use the child's spotless name to gain employment or housing.

It might be just as easy to gain a credit card for your child, too. One of her friends at Baby Cakes had laughed about her dog being sent his own credit card due to having a person-sounding name. Tyrone Labrador the Third never got a chance to use his new card due to having four legs and no opposable thumbs, which slowed him down. Never mind his fur mama cut up his card and notified the agency that issued it that he was about fifty percent Labrador and the rest suburban fence climber.

The real question centered on how the scammers got the information. Della typed in the question and waited. A plethora of companies appeared, promising to protect people from having their information lifted. One conveniently listed the ways personal details could end up in the wrong hands, the first being data breaches. Della sighed. The news featured data breaches about every other week. Most hacks were traced back to a foreign country where US authorities could do little as far as tracking down the culprits. Dumpster diving netted junk mail and sometimes more targeted mail that not only gave a person's name and address, but a few also listed birthdays, especially ones urging renewals or wishing you a happy birthday. Della made a mental note to buy a shredder and another to remember her original mental note.

The third way a person's identity could be compromised was the loss of a social security card. You'd think a person would notice that, but only if they carried it on their person, which multiplied the opportunity to lose it. Talk about a round-robin situation. It could be stolen by a clever thief who decided to help himself to personal information while visiting or robbing. Of course, those who had been robbed could put a freeze on all credit unless they didn't know they had been burgled. A subtle thief, at the most, might lift a piece of jewelry or two, open the safe, and abscond with an unused check pack. The victim would probably go weeks before using the jewelry or opening the safe and not know unless the thief started using the checks immediately, emptying out the account. The number could also be sold to those who created fake passports.

She'd read before how most identity thieves used checks to create new accounts. The Internet gave her even more information on how. Some checks even had the owner's birthday printed on them. Her mother had commented at one time that people had their social security number printed on their checks since they were often asked for it when writing a check. Others just settled for their phone number inscribed on their checks. The notion had Della shaking her head. There was no reason not to believe her mother. What stunned her was the innocence of the time. None of her friends would even use checks. There was too much information out there, but checks took longer to process. A clever thief could empty your bank account in seconds.

The article went on to list mail theft: the practice of stealing from mailboxes. Her assumption was anyone checking mailboxes hoped to nab a gift card or an ordered item of some value. They could intercept social security checks, bank statements, and even charge card statements with the full number. The last usually provided enough information to order stuff online.

Being too trusting could open a door to identity thieves, too. Salespeople, repairmen, and even dog walkers who are invited into the house could get enough information to create a fake identity. Plenty of television shows featured a person asking to use the bathroom and then going on an all-out hunt, sometimes downloading information from a computer while the homeowner waited in the next room.

Della's hand pushed through her drying hair. She winced when she saw the list continued. People had the right to be paranoid. Sometimes an identity issue could be someone with the same name. No matter how unusual a person thought their name was, a half-dozen or more people had the same name and even a few resided in the local area. Della narrowed her eyes speculatively. She'd never met anyone with *her* full name.

Using your computer in a public place allowed hackers access to your personal information and even photos. Every time a person tied into free WIFI at a public location, they were taking a chance unless their computer or phone happened to be free of all personal information. Most people knew this. At least, Della assumed they did.

The final listing made her jerk from her slumped, weary position to upright. *Phishing.* Sometimes a notice came via direct mail, email, or even text, warning you about an attack on your social security, bank account, credit card, or an online payment service using official logos, making it look authentic. A number or link would follow that claimed the victim could use to find out more but would actually be opening a way in to steal their passwords and even more information.

That one hit close to home. Just the other day, she'd gotten a special offer from her credit card agency that involved clicking on the link. Della resisted the temptation. Her father may not have been part of the cybercrime unit, but he did tell her that no officials would email or text her. When in doubt, go to the official site, drive to the local office for an in-person visit, but never blindly give away information. With caller ID, more and more people refused to answer calls from unknown numbers, forcing scammers to resort to creating realistic emails from the IRS or the FBI since people would expect to hand over personal information to such agencies.

How sad that some were taken in by such measures. Della pondered the situation, trying to understand why people would resort to such measures. Greed figured into most identity theft crimes. Sometimes, it was safer and easier for the con to steal your identity as opposed to breaking in and lifting a recently purchased wide-screen television. It was much easier buying the same wide-screen television using a credit card just issued using the victim's identity and excellent credit score. Now and then, they probably lifted someone's identity with tapped-out accounts and a lousy credit score that prevented opening any new accounts. When that occurred, they just moved on and stayed with a group that valued their good credit score.

Her phone vibrated, dancing across the table before Della could pick it up. The ring tone belonged to her mother. "Hello, Mother. I was just going to call you. The weirdest thing happened to Lorna."

"Lorna who? Never mind about that. I need to tell you what happened when I stopped to get gas and bumped into our mail lady."

# CHAPTER ELEVEN

THE TWINKLING FAIRY lights on the neighboring apartment balcony caught Della's eye as her mother's voice flowed from the phone resting on the counter. Using the speaker allowed Della to wolf down a couple of bites of her sandwich and wash it down with a swig of green tea. The simple meal tasted like ambrosia after not eating most of the day. Clowning around probably wouldn't be listed on any of those fitness apps as an activity, and if it were, they'd have it burning very few calories. Supposedly, standing burned two hundred calories per hour on the more generous calorie counter. That explained her appetite. Add in a little stress eating after chasing the hairy escapee—not to mention Lorna's peculiar phone call. Come to think of it, why did she agree to let her mother talk first?

Being the parent earned you that privilege unless something smoked and sputtered on the brink of a full-scale fire. Then the child could interrupt. Her mother rambled on about who else she had encountered on her impromptu pit stop on the way home. "I saw Declan getting gas. He looked so sad."

Knowing her mother couldn't see it, she rolled her eyes. Surely, she wouldn't go into the entire story about the man being left at the altar again. Technically, he wasn't left at the altar since the engagement ended before the two could say *I do*. Even though she attended school with both Declan and his now-defunct fiancée, she couldn't say they were ever friends.

She swallowed, able to talk. "He probably was sad. Gas jumped by about a third in the last week. Anyhow, weren't you going to tell me something incredible about your mail carrier?"

A small, affronted sniff carried over the line. "Yes, I was. Still…" Her mother paused as if trying to decide what to say next. "Declan is single. He was made partner in his accounting firm. Women will be running him down. Better jump in while the getting is good *and* while he's still vulnerable."

Geesh. Della stuck her tongue out. Somehow, her mother made the man sound a bit like a wounded raccoon—so much easier to trap, dragging his broken heart behind him. "Mother, I've never been friends with Declan. For some reason, I don't think now would be the best time to strike up a friendship. There's enough happening in my life."

"You're not holding out for Guy, are you? That man moves as fast as molasses in January."

Most liquids would move slowly in January if left outside. Besides, she and Guy really weren't a thing. Her notification chimed. Della picked up the phone to see who it was. Guy, of course—the person she didn't *really* have a relationship with.

Awkward, especially with her mother warming up for the *I want to be a grandmother before I die* rant.

She skimmed Guy's message that asked if she was free to talk. Della typed "*Will call you back,*" and then realized her mother may expect more resistance to the Declan suggestion. The sudden pause might indicate texting on her part. "Declan's not my type."

"How can you be sure?"

Why did this matter to her mother so much? Most likely, she too was hungry and tired. Della needed to redirect the conversation. "Forget about Declan. We've both lived in Owens all our lives. Plenty of time for him to fall for me, which he hasn't." Her forehead furrowed as she tried to remember any contact between the two of them. "I think the only time he talked to me was to ask me to check the school bathroom for his girlfriend."

"You're right. The man has zero interest in you. Wouldn't be a good look for you to chase after him just because he's suddenly single."

Talk about a reversal. Della's bangs ruffled as she blew out a long breath to prevent replying to her mother's statement. What could Guy want? Did he want to renegotiate their buns for cookies exchange? Maybe he called to talk. The possibility intrigued her. To talk to Guy, she'd have to fast-track the mail carrier story. "The mail carrier?"

"Oh, yeah, her." Her mother said the words as almost an afterthought. "Basically, the woman complained about a new mail app where you can see what mail is headed your way."

"That sounds like a good thing, I guess." It might be useful if someone wanted to track a rebate or a tax refund check. Still, there had to be more to it than that. "Why's your mail carrier upset about it?"

Her mother snorted. "Folks on Josie's route are complaining about things not being delivered in a timely fashion."

It didn't sound like such a big deal—certainly not worthy of bumping Lorna's break-in. "So? Why's she so upset?"

"Rumor is she was taking a little coffee break at her gentleman's house. When people mentioned that sometimes the mail is late, she got huffy and stated as long as they get it that day, it's on time."

On that point, Della would agree. Most carriers would hurry through their route to get home, but if no one waited at home, why hurry? "She has a point."

"I agree. That's not the problem. A few folks mentioned they never got the mail they saw was coming and have complained to the post office, which ticked off Josie."

"Not surprising."

"Which one? Josie being mad or people complaining?"

"Both, I guess. Do you know what failed to show up in a timely fashion?"

"Nope. Josie must have just heard about it due to her attitude. Probably shouldn't have been talking about it. You know how it is."

Her mother missed her calling as a professional bartender. People were always telling her their trials and tribulations. "I doubt anyone would complain about missing junk mail. Bills, possibly. More likely they'd notice missing ordered items, tax refund checks, rebates, or birthday cards."

"She didn't say." Her mother's voice took on a conspiratorial tone. "I *could* find out."

"Please do. Stolen mail could be used to create a false identity. I keep trying to ignore everyone complaining about their mysterious dwindling bank accounts and credit cards that don't work, trying to pretend it's somehow normal." Della shook her head. "It's hard especially after what happened to Lorna."

"Lorna?" Her mother echoed the name. "The artist?"

"No, she's the writer. You may have noticed she had a book signing at Bookmania not too long ago."

"I remember. What happened?"

Della launched into the tale with an unsettling feeling that the two of them would agree to sleuth on Lorna's behalf, which would mean no time to call back Guy. What if he had something important to ask her? If she didn't call back, it would just be bad manners. While her mouth related the details, her mind played with the idea of texting Guy. Could she text a man who wanted to talk? No, she had to call.

After she finished the tale, Della asked what she really needed to know. "Did the commissioner call?"

Her mother sighed. "Not yet. Probably not today but hopefully tomorrow."

It didn't sound like anyone would be stepping in to sort things out with the police.

"What do you think about Lorna?"

"Nasty business. At times like this, I wish your father were here. He'd know what to do."

A lengthy pause ensued. Whenever her mother talked about wishing Kenneth was here, she tended to go all quiet and melancholy. As long as her mother kept busy, she stayed relatively happy. Della knew how to keep her busy. "Maybe we could look into Lorna's attack or at the very least, a word to the right person might help."

# CHAPTER TWELVE

A S A RESULT of mentioning Lorna's incident, her mother decided they should look into it. Making sweeping decisions for everyone never fazed Mabel Delacroix. If something needed to be done, she'd do it and expect her family to follow along. For the most part, they did. Whining about it usually merited a censorious look. Her father's instructions basically mentioned something about getting it over with and all would be well. Easy for him to say because a happy wife equaled a happy life.

Even in her rebellious teenage years, refusing to wear a mermaid shirt her mother had managed to snag in an adult size may have been the pinnacle of her resistance. The mermaid on the shirt declared *All she ever wanted was to be part of a school.* Her mother thought since Della had worn a mermaid shirt on the first day of kindergarten, it would be fitting to wear a similar top a decade later. Her refusal had more to do with survival in the dog-eat-dog world of high school. One unfortunate newbie *did* make the mistake of wearing the mermaid shirt, and it didn't go well while a popular cheerleader type could have made it into a trend.

Della knew herself. She was not popular, not trendy, and not good at telling her mother no, which explained why she was shimmying into black yoga pants when she'd rather be binge-watching rom coms until she fell asleep. The falling asleep portion of the night would probably be around eight-thirty.

Her mother insisted on driving due to her car already being warmed up. Just as well, Della mused, pulling on a black, long-sleeve T-shirt. It might be all for naught despite her mother assuring her they could get into the hospital after visiting hours to check out Lorna's story. A security guard or a formidable nurse could serve as a barrier and an effective one at that. All the same, she should call Guy back right now.

Scrolling down to her recent calls, she stopped on Guy's number and hit *call*. The phone burbled a few times in her ear, just long enough to consider her greeting. They weren't close enough for a casual *Hey you*, or *It's me*.

Guy answered, "Hello?"

"Ah, yeah, hello." *Awful*. Della cringed. If she were grading her opening, she'd flunk herself. Worse yet, he might think she was a random nitwit as opposed to an intentional caller. "It's me, Della." That ought to make clear who was bumbling the conversation.

"I know. I saw your name with your number."

Ah! He put her name with her number into his phone. How sweet. The idea pleased her until she realized putting a name with a number could simply be good sense. It helped filter out the spam calls or at least you'd know which ones to answer.

"H-ha!" She forced a chuckle. "I can't fool you. Here I was going to ask if your refrigerator was running."

"Then, I'd reply yes, and you'd tell me I better go catch it."

"Something like that." At least he sounded pleased to hear from her. Should she ask why he called originally? It was kind of why she called, or maybe she should wait for him to mention it.

"I bet you're wondering what I wanted to talk about."

"Kind of why I called you back."

"Okay. Here it goes." He paused, making the interlude more dramatic. "Feel free to say no."

Feel free to say no? That's usually what people say when they mention they're moving and need help. They never want you to say *no*, hoping you'll volunteer out of pity. "You're not moving, are you?"

"No, why do you ask?"

"No reason." Would it have been better to explain or let him think she just asked weird questions out of the blue? It sounded like a disorder. Maybe they could call it random question disorder. Some television detectives operated like that—asking questions about what the guy had for dinner or what book he was reading and then could put the information together to prove his alibi fraudulent.

"All righty. My cousin is getting married, and I got my invite for myself and a plus one. I was wondering if you'd be my plus one."

Showing up at a wedding invited speculation from all the family members. "When is it?"

"Next month. Saturday the 12th, I think."

"Let me see." Someone else might be acting coy pretending to check their calendar. In Della's case, there could be a real chance she could be catering a wedding, anniversary, or making sad, angular balloon animals. She opened her calendar app and scrolled down to the next month. "I'm free. I'll need more details, though. The bakery closes at noon on Saturdays."

"Is that a yes?"

"It is."

A *whoop* sounded on the other end of the phone, which made Della grin. Still, she decided to delve a little. "Surely you might want to consider asking someone you know a little better?"

"There's no one else I'd rather go with, and I hope we might know each other a little better before the wedding rolls around."

That sounded promising. Perhaps the man did move faster than molasses on a winter day. "All right." Della typed in *wedding* on her calendar, hoping she'd remember what it was. Surely, she would. After all, it would be the first one she attended as a guest as opposed to a caterer. "Um, the wedding. It's not going to be a theme wedding, is it?"

"Theme what?"

"You know the kind where the guests have to dress in black and white or as if they're 1920s flappers."

"I hope not. If that's the case, I would rethink attending. It's my second cousin, but we're pretty close in age. We hung out at all the reunions, usually betting on what each relative would say next."

"Sounds like fun. It must be nice to have a relationship like that."

"It is. Do you have any cousins?"

"There's one or two, but none I'm close to." Look at them! They were having a perfectly normal conversation that had nothing to do with work or marketing. Now, it was her turn. Time for something clever, witty, thought-provoking, or at least flirty. "How do you come up with the name for your sandwiches?"

Guy chuckled. "Can't take a whole lot of credit since they're based on literary classic titles. When you visited, you had the Moby Dick, which turned out to be a fish sandwich. I called the bean burger Frankenburger because so many burger purists believe beans masquerading as a burger is a monstrosity." He chuckled again at his clever pun.

Della chuckled, too, but more from nervousness. She'd have to wind up the conversation before her mother showed. First, the man wants to talk, but she can't. When she does call back, she needs to cut it short. It sounded more like something from one of those books that created scenarios for women to string men along. Oddly, it worked at times.

"War and Peace. It could be called War and Pesto."

"Not really. I don't have a pesto sandwich."

"Well, you know what I mean. Anyway, I'm going to have to dash. I'm doing something with my mom."

"It's nice how you spend time with your mother. Heading out to a movie?"

That would make sense. Questioning a victim because they felt the police hadn't done a thorough enough job lacked the appropriate warm, fuzzy feelings. Most people would say they were sticking their noses in where they didn't belong. "We're going to visit a friend in the hospital."

"That's nice of you. Maybe your visit will cheer them up."

"Let's hope so." With any luck, they might get enough information to convince one of her father's coworkers that the break-in and assault had nothing to do with publicity. "Talk to you later?"

"Definitely. Bye, now."

"Bye." She hung up the phone with a tap and held it against her heart. At least something in her life was chugging along in an acceptable manner. Now, time to wrestle everything else into order.

# CHAPTER THIRTEEN

A SHARP, ANTISEPTIC smell slapped visitors as soon they entered the hospital, reminding Della a little of floor cleaner and hand sanitizer. Two nurses strolled by deep in conversation followed by a man in scrubs, clutching his phone and speaking into it in staccato phrases. Footsteps echoed in the almost empty hallway, which made it hard to believe there were dozens of patients tucked away in various rooms.

A message came over the PA system that resulted in hospital members spilling out of a lounge door and rushing off in the other direction. No one glanced at the two women dressed all in black in the corridor. Such a color fit into the dark hues people donned during the long Midwestern winter months. Who knew her mother would choose a similar outfit? It must be a Delacroix thing to don black when sleuthing.

They took the elevator to Lorna's floor and exited with little fanfare. Mabel nodded at a white-coat employee as they passed. No one confronted them. Why should they? Both she and her mother acted as though they belonged there. Her father had related tales more than once of bold thieves who wore service shirts and arrived in a panel van. Sometimes, it stated carpet cleaning and other times, plumbing. In the end, they removed everything from paintings to pianos, all on the premise of servicing it. Not too surprisingly, the items never returned.

Canned laughter flowed from slightly closed hospital room doors. Della peered at the metal name holders beside the doors. Due to regulations, the names of patients couldn't be released via the phone, but they were displayed outside the door.

"Here it is," Della offered in a low voice. "She might be asleep."

"Only one way to find out."

Mabel shaped her hand into a loose fist and delivered a spritely knock on the partially closed door. A murmured "come in" came from the other side.

They slid into the room, returning the door to its mostly closed state. At the Bookmania signing, a well made-up Lorna with an artistically arranged head of tousled curls had sat behind the table stacked with copies of her most recent book. Della blinked once, then twice, certain she had blundered into the wrong room. The woman with a three-inch line of stitches marching across a bruised forehead above a swollen, blackened eye stared back at her. The overhead lights and faded hospital gown didn't help, either. This woman probably had ten years on her school friend. "Lorna?"

"Della Delacroix. I'd recognize you anywhere. You haven't changed a bit."

Most people would consider that a good thing and possibly flush at the compliment. Della's lips twisted to one side as she tried not to think about still being the chubby, nerd girl. She forced a chuckle and gestured to her mother. "I brought my mother, Mabel."

Lorna wiggled her fingers in greeting. "I'm so sorry to drag you all here. I didn't know Mr. Delacroix was no longer with us. I just thought a word to the right person might help." A weary sigh interrupted her story. "I don't know." Her shoulders went up in a shrug. "I just have a feeling the cop who interviewed me doesn't believe me."

Mabel moved closer to the bed and patted Lorna's free hand. "It will be okay, sweetie. My husband might not be with us in the flesh, but he's with us in spirit. I know a couple of people who are still employed at the police station. I might be able to get something done."

A slight smile brightened Lorna's battered face. "That would be wonderful. What should I do?"

Mabel gave Lorna's hand a final pat before pulling up a nearby chair and sitting down. Her mother acted as if she were settling in for a good gossip. Della grabbed another chair and pushed it closer to Lorna before sitting down. Her hand dipped into her bag in search of her phone. The voice recorder app on her phone only lasted ten minutes or less. Still, a playback might allow her to catch a tidbit she might have missed by simply taking notes. Once her fingers wrapped around the phone, she held it up for Lorna to see. "Do you mind if I record?"

"Might as well. I'm not sure what difference it will make. It's the same story I told you before."

"I haven't heard it," her mother interjected.

Della almost said *yes, you have, I told you.* Thankfully, she didn't. Instead, she remembered the retelling served as a way to gather clues. Crime dramas depicted determined detectives grilling suspects by making them repeat the event over and over. Eventually they'd stumble, either changing the facts or admitting to something only the killer would know. In reality, for the victims each retelling would bring up a little more from the memory. Even though people considered themselves good eyewitnesses, they weren't, but the continual retelling helped. Sometimes, it brought up another witness or even a close circuit camera that had been previously ignored.

"Lorna, do any of your neighbors have security cameras on their homes?"

Her lips pressed together and she shook her head. "I don't know. If that was something you had, would you tell people? It would defeat the purpose."

Della nodded her head in agreement. Even though people loved the idea of it being a random stranger breaking into the house and stealing a valuable coin collection, it was more likely the culprit would be someone who knew and visited to know about it.

Her mother added, "It might not be terrible to mention it. It might just stop some behavior you wanted to stop."

"Oh! Oh!" Lorna exclaimed, slapped her forehead, and then yelped and moaned in pain. "I forgot Miss Irma."

"Miss Irma?" Della echoed the name. "Does she have a camera?"

"I'm not sure. She's a senior citizen who lives right across from me. Never goes anywhere. A bit of a busybody, but since I never do much worth noting, it doesn't bother me. Anyhow, some kids, teens I think, have been ringing doorbells and then running away. She told me she was going to get one of those doorbell cameras and catch them in the act."

With that information, they could finger the culprits in no time. They always said a picture was worth a thousand words. It had to work the same for closed-circuit cameras. A person caught committing a crime via video had to be 98.9 percent guilty, although the repeat criminals made sure to keep up their hoods or tilt their heads down to avoid being identified.

"It's possible the break-in may have triggered your neighbor's camera."

Lorna appeared thoughtful or it could just be the bruising around her eye. "Do you think the police asked her?"

If they were anything like television cops, they did. Then again, the detective might have thought this could be a stab at gathering publicity, as Lorna had mentioned on the phone.

"Not sure."

"We could ask her." At least it would be a starting point. "Who knows? We could solve this by tomorrow."

Her mother arched her eyebrows. "Woo-hoo!" Her hand went up as she half lifted from her chair. "High five!"

Della tried to slap her mother's hand, but Lorna beat her to it as she said, "That's great." Her lips tipped up into a lopsided smile and then flattened again as she shook her head. "I can't go home with those guys running around."

"No, you shouldn't," Mabel offered as she settled back into her chair. "Tell me the story from the very beginning."

Lorna's eyelids fluttered closed, making Della wonder if her friend fell asleep—understandable with the shock and whatever drugs circulated through her system. Della brought her finger to her lips and gestured to the door.

She and her mother stood ready to leave when Lorna spoke. "I can't believe it happened today. It feels like a hundred years ago. Just hours ago, I sat at my desk in my office when they broke in. I think they may have knocked first. Can't be sure. No one ever comes to see me. If anyone came knocking at my door, it would be someone trying to sell me something. All of a sudden, there was all this noise. Breaking glass."

"Breaking glass?" She hadn't mentioned this before. "What

broke?"

"Not sure. Most likely it was the glass panels beside the front door. Back when I decided to move into the house, my then-boyfriend complained anyone could break the glass and unlock the door." Lorna snorted. "Obviously, we broke up, and I forgot about it."

Mabel reached forward to touch Lorna's arm. "Don't fret about it. Hindsight is always twenty-twenty. There are dozens of things I wished I would have done." She dropped her hand and leaned back into her chair. "Go on."

"Okay." Lorna inhaled deeply and rolled her eyes. "You'd think they had to make some noise or something like jiggling the door-knob or something. I can't remember. One minute I'm chuckling to myself over a story I'm writing with a friend, and then it was glass breaking. Instead of escaping out the window, which would be the smart thing to do, I decide to see what was happening."

She paused and shook her head. "Just like one of those chicks in the slasher films who has to go look in the basement after the electricity goes out. Can't remember what I was thinking. I do remember my phone was charging in the living room. Maybe I was trying to get to my phone. By the time I reached my living room, these two men had bust in and acted surprised to see me for a second. It didn't last long. One had a crowbar, he kept swinging."

"Probably a felon," Mabel inserted. "They're not allowed to carry a gun. If they are caught committing a crime with a gun, they face stiffer sentences and higher fines. Most will use things like a pipe or even a baseball bat, something they can immediately drop. People tend to notice guns."

The hand without the IV attached went up to touch the back of her head. "I can't say I saw a gun, for which I am grateful. He certainly did a number on me with the crowbar. I dashed for the kitchen to reach the exterior door, but he tackled me from behind. Somewhere, I grabbed a skillet."

"You used it as a weapon?" Della prompted, having heard the story before.

"It may have been my plan, but I used it more as a shield. I should have used something bigger. About that time, the other guy comes in with my laptop, saying now they would be the big, famous author."

Mabel scooted to the edge of her chair. "I bet that made you angry."

"Everything went black. I assume my attacker decided to do a number on my head. The doctor told me I have a slight skull fracture along with a cracked clavicle. I woke up in a pool of blood and crawled to the living room to call 911. Then I ended up here."

"That sounds horrible," Mabel said and shook her head. "You did not deserve it, and it shouldn't have happened to you."

"Successful author, my foot. Not sure what those jerks think they can do with my laptop. There's nothing on it except the ridiculous story my friend and I were playing around with. They have no clue that being an author is a lot more than publishing stories. If I were rich and famous, I wouldn't be living where I am. They can't be the two sharpest knives in the drawer."

"I agree," Della replied.

Her mother gave her a broad wink and added, "Which means they shouldn't be too hard to catch."

# CHAPTER FOURTEEN

A GARBLED JANGLE forced Della's sleep-weighted eyes open. What now? The sound came again. For a few drowsy moments, she lay underneath her cozy, fleece blanket playing twenty questions with the noise. Was it the garbage disposal? Good heavens, no. She didn't have one. The annoying disturbance needed to stop.

A rap on her wall had her rolling over and taking her pillow with her to cover her head. Lorna might have Miss Irma, who watched everyone in the neighborhood, but Della had a second shift worker next door who hated any commotion before nine. At least, she assumed it was still before nine since she left her apartment for work well before that time. Whenever anything penetrated the thin apartment walls for more than a few seconds, she got the knocking treatment. What did he think she could do about that horrible clamor?

Oh, wait, it was her alarm. She reached over, turned it off, and groaned.

Why did morning insist on coming so early? That's what you get with a bakery. People wanted their oven-warm pastries and coffee to start their day. Five minutes more. That's all she needed. Her eyes closed and she exhaled, luxuriating in the moment. *Mustn't fall asleep*, she reminded herself as she drifted off.

A strident bird chirp awakened her, along with the pinkish predawn light playing peek-a-boo with her blinds.

Della scrambled to get out of bed and slipped on the throw rug, unceremoniously hitting the floor with a thud. On the bright side, no one witnessed her accident. The knocking quickly came from next door. Not feeling too cheery, Della pushed up to standing, then stomped a few steps. When she realized she'd only be irritating the single mother below, her footsteps softened. The stupid bird continued to chirp, which probably merited the knocking, but what could she do about a bird that for some reason sounded just like her mother's ring tone?

Talk about not operating on all cylinders. Della stumbled to her purse, retrieved her phone, and opened it. "Hello, Mother. Can't talk right now. I'm late for work."

"It's Sunday."

Della pushed her phone display to the day and time. "So it is. Wow!" She shook her head. "If I showed up at work, at least there'd be no one there to tease me."

"If they were there, they'd be guilty of showing up on a Sunday, too. What time did you get to bed? You sound tired."

Della scratched her head, trying to remember. "It had to be after eleven. I found myself searching the Internet for anyone who had tried to impersonate a famous writer."

"Did you find anything?"

"Some but not anything like Lorna's story. One successful author who never made public appearances suddenly started to show up in public, only it wasn't her. An opportunistic woman had passed herself off as the author. She attended signings, gave interviews, and allowed people to host parties in her honor—the whole shebang."

"If you read about it, then she was caught. Who blew the whistle on her?"

"Actually, the author happened to be a man but used a female pen name. He felt no one would take a male romance author seriously. I doubt the impersonator received money, just her fifteen minutes of fame at the bookstore and the courtroom."

"I'm not sure what the benefit of that was. Maybe a brush with fame. We need someone who makes money off the famous scribblers. Find some of those."

"Not as easy. We have the usual, digital piracy issue with folks based in foreign countries lifting the books and pocketing the proceeds. There're also people who rewrite current popular books, merely changing the characters and the location. Often these books go to press without anyone noticing immediately, demonstrating those in the publishing field are not as well read as you might suspect. How about you? You find anything out?"

"You're in luck. Delores, the dispatcher, didn't mind my calling so late last night. We had a good chat, and I told her about Lorna. She knew about the case and confirmed what I already thought. The out-of-town detective is working on it. None of our own would treat a citizen with so much discourtesy. That's the good news."

Sure, Della had missed out on her eight hours of rest but having Detective Snide on a case couldn't be good. "What's the bad news?"

"As you guessed, the big city cop refused to take Lorna's complaint seriously. Who beats themselves with a crowbar for promotion purposes? A faked kidnapping would work for that—nothing to detract from her looks."

"Bad news," she prompted, afraid her mother might go off on a tangent about fake crimes where a person could still look good as a victim with no one questioning it.

"Oh, yeah, that." A grumbling sound carried over the phone. "Thanks to Big City Detective, the crime scene became compromised by neighbors coming by for a look-see. For some reason, he failed to call it in immediately. Apparently, the commissioner heard about it and pulled him from the case. That's the good news."

"That *is* good. That's why you called?"

"Sort of." Her mother cleared her throat. "There's a manpower shortage so our CSI unit, or what little we have that passes for one, won't be over to Lorna's place until this afternoon."

"Okay." Why her mother thought this information would interest her puzzled her. "This is important, why?"

"It gives us plenty of time to go over and look ourselves." Her mother's tone indicated the answer should be obvious to anyone.

"We'd be just as bad as the neighbors who contaminated the scene."

Her mother snorted. "Drink some coffee. You're not thinking straight. We're practically professionals and will be honing our sleuthing skills."

# CHAPTER FIFTEEN

ELLA WENT THROUGH the motions of dressing and donning a ball cap with a service company logo on it, while the idea of examining a crime scene on her only free day held no allure. What could they possibly do at a crime scene? Sure, her father had been a detective, but even detectives weren't blood spatter experts. It usually required a degree and at least three years of experience before being certified.

The delay in getting forensics over there could be explained by not having an actual CSI team. More likely, the team at Centerville would come in and process the scene much to the irritation of Owens' finest. What in the world did her mother plan to do that the experts couldn't?

Would they take talcum powder and cellophane tape, the way she did when she was ten and played at being a girl detective? Her father made sure to touch several areas, making plenty of prints to dust and pull. Della prided herself on her ability to pull prints without adding her own, but in the end, whatever prints they could pull wouldn't matter. They had no way to test the fingerprints against a database. Trying to identify them would be useless. Nothing good could come from the effort. She'd have to call her mother and beg off.

Her nose crinkled as she considered the results. Any person

other than her mother would be disheartened and call off running the escapade on her own. Her stomach rolled because Della knew better. Once Mabel Delacroix got an idea in her head, there'd be no dissuading her. If Della refused to participate, her mother would push on. If anything happened, it would be Della's fault. As the only child, she should guard her mother against hurting herself. She, however, would never make the mistake of saying as much aloud.

Her phone already in her hand, she set it on silent to guard against irritating her neighbor. To be fair, most of the time she never heard or saw her neighbor—just the occasional knocking let her know someone lived on the other side of the wall. A chance comment by another neighbor about the man working second shift explained his dislike of early morning sounds. Della's phone vibrated. "Who, now?"

She pulled the phone out of her pocket, resolving that if another person called to ask for her help, it would be a definite *no*. Then she saw her mother's name. "Hello. You called to tell me you've reconsidered our evidence sweep?"

"Oh, no. I'm outside your apartment."

She couldn't be. Della opened the exterior door, walked to the outside stairs, squatted, and peered down into the parking lot. A familiar sedan with lights on and engine running waited at the bottom of the stairs. Della spoke into the phone as she hurried to get her purse and jacket. "How did you get here so quick?"

"Called you while I was on my way. I gave you enough time to dress, but not enough time to overthink everything."

As an expert in overthinking everything, Della didn't need much time to do so. She locked up the apartment and proceeded down the stairs, aware she'd been manipulated. Well, two could play that game. She climbed into the car and announced, "I'd love to take you to the lady's brunch at the Evergreen Hotel."

Her mother had talked incessantly about the fussy brunch with ice sculptures, crepes, fresh flowers on every table, and fresh fruit salad in champagne glasses ever since the Evergreen started advertising it almost a decade ago. Her father tried to take her a couple of times, but work had interfered. The brunch could be an elegant exit from a tricky conundrum.

"I'd love to go," her mother answered with a wide smile while Della buckled up and closed the door.

Talk about easy. Here she worried about disappointing her mother, who probably imagined herself as one of her favorite fictional detectives on a big case. All she needed was a keen mind and an oversized magnifying glass to solve the crime. Even her father admitted her mother not only possessed a keen mind but remembered everything. Sometimes, the storage system left a little something to be desired.

The smooth voice of the GPS prompted a left turn that would be coming up in a quarter mile. If they turned left, they'd be driving away from downtown and the hotel. Then again, navigation systems seldom took a direct route.

Still, she decided to comment. "This isn't the way to the Evergreen Hotel."

"You're right." Mabel kept her gaze straight ahead as she headed out of town and toward the suburbs that ringed the town of Owens. "You think they'd let you into the ladies brunch dressed like that?"

What might work in a gym or cleaning out a basement would invite censure from brunch attendees in their Sunday best. "I can change. Turn around. For you, I'll put on a dress."

"Whoo, fancy," her mother teased but showed no signs of changing her direction.

"Don't you want to go to the ladies' brunch?" When she offered her mother the one thing she thought her mother wanted but got marginal interest, it perplexed her. Clothes could easily be changed. "I'll slap on some makeup, too."

"That's sweet of you. It's seven in the morning, which is the opposite of brunch. When you wake up at almost noon and want mimosas with your omelet, then that's brunch."

Good point. An almost afternoon brunch would offer no solution as far as steering her mother away from the morning crime scene inspection. "Maybe we can go later."

"I wish." Her mother sighed. "They haven't had brunch for about two or three years. Owens doesn't have enough ladies who brunch." She chortled. "You heard what I did there with the phrase, right? Ladies who brunch as opposed to ladies who lunch."

"I did. At the very least, we should get some coffee. You wrestled me out of the apartment before I even had breakfast."

"Work first, then breakfast. We can go to the pancake house. They're still serving pumpkin pancakes, and they have caramel syrup, too."

Her mother's weakness might be fancy brunches, but Della would settle for pumpkin pancakes every time. "I guess we could do that. We'll have to be quick. In and out of Lorna's place. No touching anything. What are we looking for?"

"Anything that will help identify the home invaders."

"Like a wallet complete with a driver's license and grocery store loyalty card," Della joked. She considered finding anything useful to be unlikely. Still, things get dropped. Criminals aren't the masterminds you see on television shows that required multiple episodes to catch the would-be felon.

"A wallet would be super." She turned to address Della before facing the road again. "I see you made a funny."

"I did." Might as well change the subject. "How about the commissioner?"

"He's okay. Kind of cute in that weathered leather fashion. You know what I mean?"

She didn't. Men who bore a resemblance to weathered leather sounded more like purse material as opposed to boyfriends. "I meant did he call you?"

"Not yet. Even though we've stayed busy, it's been twelve hours and part of that time I spent sleeping. Maybe today. All the more reason to get in and out. Call Lorna and ask her if she needs us to take her anything."

"She's getting out today."

"Nope. She *thinks* she's getting out today. No doctor is coming in just to sign her out. Remember, my best friend is Clarice, a nurse who has spent decades working at the hospital, which means I know how things operate. Call her now for me."

"She could be sleeping." After suffering the trauma, sleep might be her only escape.

"We need an excuse as to why we're at her house. Someone will ask. They always do."

Otherwise, it might be mistaken for breaking and entering. She chose to text as opposed to calling. A drowsing person could nap through a text notification. *Anything we can run by your house and get for you?*

Since Lorna believed she'd be going home today, she'd probably say nothing. But a message came back quickly. *Get me some real pajamas. Blue ones in my white dresser top drawer will do. Grab the book on my nightstand. I am so bored. Thanks, friend.*

The friend label felt unearned since her intention centered on snooping as opposed to being helpful. *Will do*, she typed back.

They pulled up to a modest duplex with crime scene tape across the broken door and trampled shrubs. Della wondered if the shrub abuse came more from the looky-loo neighbors as opposed to Lorna's attackers.

No one was moving around in the neighborhood, which worked in their favor. Perhaps most still slumbered, exhausted from yesterday's excitement. With no reason not to park near the house, Mabel pulled up in front of the crime scene.

As soon as they opened the car doors, an elderly woman popped out of the house across the street, reminiscent of one of those clocks that had figurines pop out on the hour. This must be Miss Irma, the woman Lorna had mentioned.

Miss Irma approached the car at a surprisingly fast march for a person of her advanced age, and she held her chin a little higher than natural. Once she reached the car doors which were swung open, the woman put out both palms. "Stop! You're not going anywhere. This is a crime scene. If you drove across town to nib in other's misfortune, you are sad excuses for humans."

Her friend forgot to mention her neighbor's protective nature. No one had ever come down on Della that hard. Before she could say anything, her mother slid from the car. "Oh my, we would never do such a thing. My daughter is a friend of Lorna's."

She gestured to Della, who stood on cue. Maybe she was supposed to say something, too. "Lorna asked me to bring her pajamas and a book. She's bored at the hospital."

The woman's eyes narrowed as she processed the statement. "That could be true. I'll guide you in to make sure you do what you say you came to do."

It was not exactly what they came to do, but there was not much else they could do without drawing suspicion to themselves. Della closed her car door and followed the woman, who led them to the back door. She stopped, caught up her shirt hem, covered the doorknob with it, and opened the door. "Prevents fingerprinting."

Ah, yes it did and smeared any other fingerprints, and Della couldn't help noticing the unlocked condition of the door. She followed without comment past paper towels littering the floor. Her mother failed to use the same restraint.

"What's with the paper towels?"

"Blood. Couldn't stand seeing it. I know head wounds bleed a lot." She patted the area above her heart. "It breaks my heart knowing the poor girl laid on the floor bleeding and alone."

It nudged Della's memory to ask about the doorbell camera. "You think anyone had a doorbell camera and got some footage of the bad guys?"

"Don't know. I bought one, but never had it installed."

There went one sure bet. "Do you need help putting it in?"

"My nephew promised to come by and install it. After yesterday's horrible incident, he should come by today. By the way, I'm Miss Irma."

"Della. My mother's Mabel Delacroix."

They skirted the paper towels where a discarded frying pan rested against the wall. The red pan had a sizeable dent, which might fit the skull of the culprit. No way could they grab it casually as they left with the pajamas. With any luck, the police might pick it up as a clue. As they moved past the living room with furniture turned over and broken glass, Della imagined the panic her old friend must have felt. Her breath caught. How horrible.

Miss Irma cleared her throat and gestured to the hall. "The bedroom is back here."

The implication was she should follow, and she did, but not so her mother. It only took a few minutes to find the pajamas and book in a glorified closet of a room.

The sound of car doors slamming had Irma hurrying to the back door to stop any more unexpected visitors. She passed Mabel, failing to see she was in the process of tucking a plastic bag into her pocket.

Irma swung the back door open. A uniformed officer stood there beside a frowning commissioner, who asked, "What are you doing here?"

"Helping these ladies get some stuff for Lorna." Irma acted like it was the most normal thing in the world.

Della made sure to hold up the pajamas and book. The commissioner worked his chin back and forth and then glanced over at Mabel. "I'll talk to *you* later."

He gestured for them to leave, which the three of them did, scurrying like mice. They thanked Irma outside the unit and then climbed into the car and left. After driving for a few minutes, her mother glanced into the rear-view mirror before remarking, "I don't think I'm a fan of weathered leather."

Della would bet her mother's dislike of weathered leather would increase, especially after a certain phone call to keep his promise to talk to her later.

# CHAPTER SIXTEEN

SILVERWARE SCRAPED AGAINST china while conversation flowed around Della and Mabel along with the heady aroma of coffee and caramel syrup. Della took a hefty bite of her pumpkin pancakes, chewed, and sighed in contentment. "This is *so* good."

"You deserve it. I know you didn't want to go to Lorna's place."

"True," she acknowledged, cutting off another bite. "We really need to get to the hospital. We might as well deliver Lorna's pajamas while she can still use them. Should we say anything about her house?"

Her mother's brows knitted as she swallowed a mouthful of coffee, and she gave a small shake of her head. "No reason to mention the place being trashed. Either she already knows or it would be just one more shock on top of another. When she returns home, she'll have to deal with it."

"I just wish there was something more we could do as far as nabbing the culprits." Della squirmed in her seat, wishing she could do something or at least find the smoking gun—so to speak. "What did you bag in the house?"

Her mother held up a finger. "Wait." She pawed through her purse and retrieved a plastic bag filled with a cylinder-shaped object inside. "What do you think this is?"

Della accepted the plastic bag and examined the iridescent metallic object. It was thicker than a pen, more like a metal cigar with a tip, and had a button on one side. "Not sure. It reminds me of one of those devices from sci-fi movies that wipes people's memories."

"Nah…" they both said in tandem and laughed.

It had to be something, but would it be the clue to break the case? Her mother signaled the server for the bill while Della continued to stare at the object, willing it to tell her what it was.

"You know," Della started, holding the bag by the edges so as to not smear any possible fingerprints. "I had a co-worker who had a severe bee allergy. She carried an EpiPen with her. This doesn't look like an EpiPen since there's no needle, but maybe it's a medical device. If so, and we figure out what it's used for and find a former felon with the same medical issue, we'll have a trail."

"You're the best," Mabel cooed and slapped her hands together. "All we need to do is show it to Clarice. She'll know what it is."

The server chose that moment to stroll to their table with the coffee pot and their bill. She glanced at the bag Della held by the edge and commented, "Pretty. I got sucked in, too, by all the advertising and low price." She put down the check and pointed to the bag. "You're better off not vaping. Sure, people think it is better than smoking, but the trade-offs…" She clicked her tongue before continuing. "They are so not worth it. My vape pen ruined a brand-new purse by leaking."

"So sorry to hear that," her mother commiserated as she removed her debit card from her wallet. "You can get a decent purse at the consignment store on Maple."

"That's what I heard," the server agreed, before bustling off to a nearby patron who held up what must be an empty coffee cup.

"Well…" Della said as she handed the bagged vape pen back to her mother. "Now that we know what it is, there's no reason to see Clarice."

Her mother pouted and pushed to a standing position. "I guess it would have been too easy, just like finding a wallet with identification. I heard on one of those true crime podcasts they solved a murder by finding a flashlight. Apparently, it was sold in a two-pack set and the purchase was traced back to the murderer."

"Not sure we can trace a vape pen back to a particular person. After all, there's so many of them in circulation."

Her mother cleared her throat and whispered, "Wait, I got it! I'll tell you in the car. No need for anyone to hear us and alert the thugs."

If anyone had bothered listening and happened to be associated with the would-be famous authors, they'd know both she and her mother were clueless, which would be all they could pass on. Still, in a town numbering under twenty thousand, she expected the odds of being in the same place with friends of Lorna's home invaders to be minuscule at best. Her mother practically trembled with anticipation as she headed toward the cashier station.

Della pulled off a couple of fives and placed them on the table. The helpful server deserved a good tip. She probably saved them a couple of hours with Clarice rehashing all the hospital gossip before telling them what the object was. By the time she reached the pay station, her mother was visibly upset, speaking to the cashier through tight lips, "I'm not sure what is wrong. I know I have money in the bank."

Not her mother, too! Della, fortunately, had cash on her and handed over a twenty. "I think this will cover it."

The cashier shot her a grateful smile as she took the offered bill.

"Yes, it will." She popped open the cash drawer, placed the bill on the corner, then counted out coin change. "You have thirty-eight-cents change."

"Put it in the penny pan." She waved the change away with a smile and guided her mother outside.

Away from prying, local ears, her mother babbled. "You know me. I keep a tight watch on the bank balance."

"I know you do," Della reassured as she herded her mother to the passenger side. No way would she let her upset parent drive. Studies showed that driving while upset often proved to be as dangerous as driving drunk. "Dad used to joke you had him on an allowance."

The comment caused Mabel's worried mien to smooth out at the mention of her husband and a wistful expression replaced it. "Not an allowance, per se. More like a budget. Your father could go through money. He was way too generous. He'd go out with friends and want to buy everyone lunch. Every kid that sold something, he had to buy it. I have a closet full of wrapping paper rolls never opened. Don't get me started on those restaurant cards that are usually for only a certain item at a specific time and are never applicable when you actually do go."

"I'll have to hit you up for the wrapping paper sometime."

"Please do." Della held her hands out for the keys.

Her mother sighed heavily. "You're treating me like a child."

"Children don't drive."

"My point."

"At least let me drive you to the bank."

Her mother cocked her head to one side and wrinkled her nose. "You do know it's Sunday."

"That's what you keep telling me. We can go to the ATM, and it will show your last ten transactions. Maybe we can track down the problem."

After obtaining the keys, Della hurried over to the driver's side. Thankfully, a branch of her mother's bank sat only a few blocks away. She started the car and exited the park without any conversation, both women engaged in their own interior dialogues. While lots of locals dealt with financial issues, she knew her mother. For as long as she could remember, her mother balanced her bank statement with her readers perched on her nose and a calculator at hand. She even insisted on teaching Della how when she was in sixth grade. While some folks might consider her mother's cheerful manner indicated a mental lightweight, they'd be the ones fooled when it came to Mabel Delacroix's bookkeeping skills, which were second to none.

"It could be just a fluke," Della addressed the words to her mother, not totally believing them herself. "I've had that happen. I can't get gas at one station with my debit card, go to another, and I'm fine."

Her mother snorted. "You don't really believe that after everything else that has happened?"

"No. I was trying to reassure you, but that was always your job." She managed a forced smile. "I guess I'm not particularly good at it. What were you going to tell me about the vape pen in the restaurant?"

"Ah, I see what you did there. Changed the subject. Another great strategy." Her mother inhaled, glanced out the window, and pointed, "There's my bank."

"I see it." Della flipped on her blinker. "That's where I was headed." She chose not to comment on her mother's habit of mentioning the obvious. "Your vape comment? It had something to do with the vape pen, and you didn't want people to overhear."

"Oh, that." Her mother had a good grip on her purse, ready to vault out of the car as soon as Della pulled up to the lobby ATM. "DNA. There could be DNA on the vape pen."

"Excellent." Della slowed, braked, and then parked. "His DNA could be on the pen. If he's ever been arrested, it's possible his DNA would be on file. Of course, that means the police need to have the pen to run the test."

Her mother, instead of answering her, dashed out of the car and into the exterior lobby where an ATM waited. A young mother with a stunned expression exited, clutching the hand of a young child. The sight caused some speculation on the possibility of the mother just experiencing a financial shock like her own parent. Even though her mother probably wouldn't welcome her assistance, Della chose to check on how things were going.

Inside the small, overheated entry area that smelled of mints and old coffee, her mother stared at the ATM with pursed lips. "What's wrong?"

"My account's been frozen."

Della peered around her mother to read the screen. In bold letters it announced *wrong password attempt 3x, resulting in freezing the account. Must see a bank representative during normal working hours to unfreeze it.*

"Okay. Have you been trying to access your account?"

"No, not until I tried to pay for breakfast."

Well, obviously someone had been trying to get into her mother's account. "Do you have any password hints?"

"Everybody does."

Hackers liked to brag about people having obvious passwords like their birth date or the name of their child or pet. It could be password hints were just as easy. "What are your hints?"

Her mother turned to face Della and mouthed, "Not here."

Sure, they were on camera. Her mother showed good sense not to answer. They both climbed into the car, with Della maintaining the driver's place. Once the doors were closed, her mother insisted on turning on the radio, as if assuming there had to be a recording device nearby. Plenty of skimmers were attached to bank card readers and sometimes ATMs. It wouldn't be too much of a stretch to attach a recording mechanism. From what she'd read, thieves who installed the skimmer returned to pick up the device before it was detected. The stored ATM and credit card information was used immediately by the skimmers online to get as much as they could before the theft was discovered.

Most of the time, skimmers are used on the weekends due to people needing cash and banks being closed. Come Monday morning, every bank machine would receive a thorough inspection.

"I think you're safe to speak."

"All right. My first hint is what was my first car?"

"A Ford Focus," Della guessed, having heard stories about her mother's first car.

"Oh, no, that would make it too easy. On the hint questions, you have to give the wrong answer. Simple small talk could be a gold mine of hint information if a person put real answers down. My answer was a Cortina."

"Cortina? Never heard of it."

"That's why it's a good answer. It's a Ford car made exclusively for the UK. I guess with the steering wheel on the other side, it wouldn't be much good here."

"Makes sense. All your answers to your password hints are wrong?"

"Absolutely. Your father insisted." She gave an emphatic nod. "At the time, I thought it silly, but his suggestion came just about the time Internet banking came on the scene."

Her father had been a bit of a digital security visionary. "Smart of him. That means whoever attempted to get into your account failed. It makes me wonder. Our thief felt cocky enough to try passwords or passwords hints, feeling like he should know or guess them. I wonder if this is what others are experiencing."

"We should drop by Clarice's right after we see Lorna."

The visit Della thought she had dodged but hadn't.

# CHAPTER SEVENTEEN

THE PUMPKIN PANCAKES sat like a brick in Della's stomach as she drove to the hospital. Her mother decided to call Clarice, worried someone or maybe someones were trying to pry her bank account open. It couldn't be called eavesdropping if the person rode in the car with you and spoke loudly.

"Did you give out your information to anyone?" Mabel questioned her friend.

Even though Della heard only her mother's side of the conversation, she could follow it well enough. Her mother made a derisive snort. "Not that. I doubt the brow specialist at the Beauty Barn is trying to steal your identity. Something like maybe an investment firm or medical form you filled out recently."

Her mother sighed. "Yes, I know. As a nurse, you wouldn't be filling out any medical paperwork since you visit your own facility for services. The reason I asked is someone tried to break into my account. I'm trying to find out what everyone who's recently had money trouble has in common…Very funny," her mother said in a not amused manner.

The last comment piqued Della's curiosity. "What did she say?"

"Lack of money causes the money troubles."

Della rolled her eyes. That sounded like Clarice. "It's more like lack of *access* to the money."

"True enough. We need to put a stop to it." Mabel turned to her phone. "No, not you, I don't expect *you* to do anything." She paused, possibly considering what a gossip powerhouse her friend was. "You could keep your ears open for anyone suffering money issues but puzzled by it. Lots of people overdraw their bank account but know why. Listen for folks genuinely stunned." Her mother waited for a few minutes and then said, "I appreciate it."

If Clarice started snooping around, nothing would stay secret for long. "Mother, you know if the culprits hear folks are asking questions, they'll stop."

"Is that such a bad thing?"

Della knew a rhetorical question when she heard one. Sure, it would be good to have their identity thieves move elsewhere, but not before they received punishment for their misdeeds in disrupting the lives of Owens' citizens.

Instead of responding immediately, she turned into the hospital parking lot. "We should table our conversation topic before we go inside, since we don't know who our culprits are."

Her mother's face puckered up as if she'd bitten into an unripe persimmon. "Oh, honey, I don't like to think it's local. It's not someone I went to school with or see at the grocery."

No one considered people that they encountered every day as they stood in line at the post office and chatted about the weather could be probing to see how easy it would be to steal their identity or if it would even be worth the effort. When a few boys in her senior class decided to switch license plates all through town as a prank, no one pointed the finger at them. No student wanted to be labeled a squealer, and none of the adults believed anyone in Owens could be the cause.

She understood her mother's reluctance to believe the worst of any of Owens' citizens. After the unthinkable loss of her husband, Mabel Delacroix clung to the All-American image of her small town. As a good daughter, she assured her parent, "You're right. It has to be an out-of-towner. Who knows? Financial strings could be pulled from abroad."

"That's right." Her mother brightened at the possibility. "The only problem with that is it would be hard to prosecute. Lorna would be terrified to go home."

Della parked the car in the visitor section, noting the sparsity of cars. After tucking the pajamas and book into her tote bag, she eased out of the car. Light rain gave the pavement a shiny appearance, which could be slippery. Not a one to take chances, she hurried around to lock her arm with her mother's.

Mabel gave a slight tug to free her arm while muttering, "I'm not a creaky fossil who can't toddle into the hospital on my own speed."

"Maybe *I* need the help, not you."

"Yeah, sure."

"I wanted to talk but not be overheard."

"Oh." Her mother intertwined her arm with Della's. "Why didn't you say so?"

"I just did." Even though the closest person just disappeared inside the emergency room, security still mattered. Too many trusting people had allowed important information to slip. "When we see Lorna, don't mention anything about locals suffering identity theft."

"Why not? The two could be connected. If we find one, we could find the other." Her shoulders went up in a shrug. "It might make her feel better knowing others are suffering, too. There's a German word for it, I think."

"Schadenfreude. It means taking joy from other's misfortune. It doesn't fit here. I think it only applies if the other person experiencing the pain is particularly deserving. Anyhow, Lorna's attackers' snatch and grab behavior isn't exactly criminal mastermind stuff. I have a hunch that whoever is fiddling with bank accounts has to have a little more on the ball. Let's try to be upbeat. I wish we had brought something nice like chocolate or flowers."

"There's a gift shop inside," her mother pointed out as they strolled toward the entrance doors.

Ten minutes later, they stood inside Lorna's hospital room with Della clutching a pink bear with an *It's a Girl* ribbon tied around its neck, while Mabel held the string of a yellow smiley face balloon.

Lorna welcomed them with a smile. "You're the best thing I've seen this morning. You're practically the *only* people I've seen. Once I started asking when I'd be getting out, it's like I have leprosy the way everyone keeps their distance."

Mabel caught her daughter's eye and inclined her head slightly. Score one for her mother, not too surprising with her buddy working in the hospital. Lorna would not be released today. After delivering the gifts and requested items, the three of them sat around and chatted about inconsequential things, avoiding the obvious.

Finally, Lorna gave a weary sigh. "How's my house look?"

"It's a mess," Della admitted, following her father's advice to keep it simple when delivering unwelcome news. "Nothing that can't be cleaned up. Police have to do their bit, and then you can put everything back to normal."

"Normal," Lorna echoed the word and groaned. "I don't even know what *normal* is anymore. Besides, I can't go back home. I know I have to, but I don't feel safe there. My front door can be pried open as easily as a pop-top on a can."

"Parents?" Mabel asked, assuming it would be the natural place to go. "How about your mother?"

What Della heard was *where is your mother and why isn't she here clucking over you*? Apparently, Lorna didn't hear the underlying message. She responded to the first question. "My parents moved to Florida about three years ago. Dad died about eight months later due to an aneurysm. About a year later, my mother married Damon."

The way she spat out the name said the two of them didn't have a cordial relationship. Della decided to not touch the subject. The emotions seething under that name could serve as a starting flag for the release of a myriad of negative connotations.

While most folks would avoid saying anything, not her mother. "Damon? I'm not familiar with that name. Not from Owens?"

"No, he's a Florida man. Not sure if I'd call him a man. *Dictator* is more like it. I didn't call my mother because she'd be worried. Damon wouldn't let her come because who would fetch and carry for him? My mother would be suffering in Florida while I sat in the hospital here. Why should we both be miserable?"

A sympathetic clucking issued from Mabel as she pawed through her purse, putting various items on the bed including the bagged vape pen. "Aha! I found it." She waved a small card case.

Della recognized her father's card case. It contained business cards her father had passed out to victims, possible suspects, and informants alike. The number on the card no longer worked. Why did her mother carry it around, other than for sentimental reasons? Better yet, why did she pull it out for Lorna?

Rather than responding to Mabel's *aha* moment, Lorna fingered the bagged vape pen. "Why did you bring my vape? They won't allow vaping inside the hospital."

So much for their great clue and easy DNA trail to the culprits. Her mother slumped in the chair like a balloon losing air. Yes, she had definitely heard Lorna's remark. Her mother reached for a pen, extracted a card from a case, wrote on it, and handed it to Lorna.

"Here's my phone number and address. You can stay with me."

"Oh, no, I couldn't do that," Lorna refused the invitation but not too hard.

Her mother's invitations weren't casually offered up. In fact, her mother *never* invited anyone else to camp out at the family residence.

"Go," Della encouraged. "It won't be too long. Besides, you can meet my brother, Tony. He's an attention hog."

"You have a brother?" Lorna's eyes grew large while she possibly imagining a thirty-something man refusing to move out of the parental home.

"Tony's a dog."

"Oh, really?" Lorna scooted up a little straighter in bed. "I'd like that. I keep saying I need a dog. Maybe living with Tony will help me decide."

"It's a deal." Mabel clapped her hands together and beamed. "I won't be home during the day due to helping at the bakery, but you'll have Tony for company. Best of all, no one will know where you are."

Normally, the no one knowing where you were functioned as the heavy or the bad guy's line, but Della knew better than to mention it. When a nurse entered to take vitals, they excused themselves, reminding Lorna to call when she needed a ride.

As she and her mother waited for the elevator, her mother stomped one foot. "Gee whiz! I thought the vape pen would be the clue we needed."

"Too easy. On the other hand, you won't have to turn it over to old leather face."

"*Weathered* leather face," her mother corrected. "This puts us back to the starting line with no real evidence."

# CHAPTER EIGHTEEN

THE OVEN BUZZER sounded as Della donned her oven gloves. Her nose had already alerted her that the double chocolate cupcakes needed to come out. Chocolate required a delicate hand since it could dry out so easily. Usually, her nose could differentiate between not done and about ten seconds away from being too done.

Heat blasted her as she opened the oven doors. For a moment, the rich chocolate aroma embraced her before dissipating. If she could bottle that, people would line up to buy it.

She moved the hot cupcakes to the counter to cool, then inserted the waiting pans into the oven. Her decision to add cupcakes to her sugary line-up took off like wildfire. Many people somehow talked themselves out of a cookie but fell under the spell of an iced cupcake. Why not? They were like a tiny party that could be consumed in three or four bites, lessening the guilt. A cupcake rated as a lesser extravagance than a whole cake or a dozen cookies. Surprisingly, some of her morning customers returned for a midday cupcake. Their loyalty should be rewarded.

"Steph!" she called out to her morning helper. "Do you think we should get some type of reward card? Such as buy seven cups of coffee, get the eighth one free?"

The helper in question walked into the kitchen, wiping her hands on a tea towel. Stephanie sucked in her lips and released them with a popping sound. "Your idea has potential, but you need to make it 21$^{st}$ century friendly."

They *were* living in the 21$^{st}$ century. Della smiled as she used a fork to pop the cupcakes out of the pan, exposing paper wrappers decorated with hearts and arrows. It was perfect for her bakery. Never mind they were left over from Valentine's Day. She pretended not to notice Stephanie edging her way closer to the cupcakes.

"What do you mean by 21$^{st}$ century?"

"No cards people have to produce whenever they stop in. Every-one loses those after the first punch or before they're almost finished. No one ever gets the advantage of the card. They might have purchased seven coffees, but only have six or less on their card before misplacing it."

There was no need to mention Della kept track of all her loyalty cards and cashed them in. "Most people wouldn't notice if they were a cup or two behind. I agree there has to be a better system. Any suggestions?"

"Glad you asked," Stephanie replied but her focus dropped to the cooling cupcakes.

"Go ahead." Something about working in a bakery turned adults into children when it came to fresh-baked goodies. Once her helper bit into the cupcake, Della teased her. "Tell me your idea first."

Stephanie sputtered with a mouthful of cupcake. "Unfair."

"Possibly," Della replied with a grin. "You'd best chew and swal-low." She busied herself arranging cookies on a display tray as Stephanie finished her treat.

"When I first walked back here, I was thinking something like a grocery loyalty card you swipe to keep track of visits. While that has some benefits, people forget those cards, too. Then I realized my grocery has an alternative ID, which is your phone number. We could have people make an account and when they visit, all they'd have to do is type in their number. That way we'd have their phone number, too."

Stephanie's streamlined plan would work easier than her paper card one. Still, it surprised her that people would easily give up their phone numbers. "Won't customers object to giving up their phone numbers?"

A mouthful of cupcake again, Stephanie settled on swinging her head side to side. After swallowing, she added, "Plenty of people use their phone number to sign up for loyalty rewards."

Good point. Della should know. A half-dozen or more cards crowded her wallet and a few more populated her key ring. "Maybe we could get their birthday and remind them to come in for a free birthday treat."

"Now you're cooking with gas."

Della shot her employee a confused look while Stephanie shrugged before explaining further. "Something my mom says whenever someone comes up with something good. I'm not sure where it came from. Your idea is a good one. People like to get free stuff on their birthdays. It makes them feel special."

Stephanie crossed her arms and raised her chin slightly. "You'd be amazed what someone will do if they think they might get something free or win something. Sure, they'll give away their email address, phone number, and home address, in hopes of getting a free dessert at local restaurants on their birthdays, and then complain about all the junk mail and phone calls they get when the information is sold."

Della's eyes widened. "We don't want to sell information. That's dastardly."

"I don't know about dastardly, but it's done all the time. We could make sure to include a line on the application about not selling information. That should reassure people. Since we'd have phone numbers, we could send out texts about sales."

Della wrinkled her nose, not so much about the sales text, but about how freely people gave up information. "You're saying people will give us their name, phone number, birth date, and possibly email address for a free coffee or cookie?"

"Yep." Stephanie licked her fingers and narrowed her eyes as she did so. "Your voice went all funny. What were you thinking when you said that?"

"Identity theft."

"Not cool." Stephanie displayed her palms as if to stop whatever might come next. "I thought the bakery was in the black."

"Please." She snorted, reminiscent of her mother. "Not something I'm thinking of doing, but I'm curious as to how it's done. People who have their identity stolen aren't on the street corner handing out their identification. The pertinent data must leave them in a socially acceptable way, like signing up for a loyalty card, for example."

Bending her index finger, Stephanie used the knuckle to rub at her brow. "I don't know. Sure, people are giving away info all the time. Your name, people must know that. Your address is public knowledge from the people at the courthouse to your mail carrier. Email isn't that great unless it's used for a phishing scheme."

Stephanie straightened her finger and wagged it. "Now, the phone number's a little trickier to get since most people who have cell service don't want to get a bunch of spam calls. I'm not sure how that would help someone impersonate someone else."

"Not sure, either," Della admitted. "More than a few people are having issues with their money flow. It's not the usual issue of overspending. My mother and I figure someone is dipping into their bank accounts or at least trying."

"Geesh. Uncle Wilbur might get the last laugh. Too bad he's dead and can't enjoy it."

Every now and then, Stephanie would throw out an odd comment that confused Della. "Uncle Wilbur?"

"Great uncle. Kept his money in a sock under his mattress. He didn't trust banks. Something about the Depression and banks not paying out the money put into them. Anyhow, if he were alive today, he'd tell everyone I told you so."

American history class had hinted at the masses having a similar attitude. That much Della remembered along with men riding the rails in freight cars in an effort to find work. Still, blaming a faceless institution served those who felt powerless. "It's not the bank's fault. They're just a third party holding the sums. Rather like a blindfolded third party who believes whoever comes up and asks for money."

"They should be more careful." Stephanie put her hand on the counter near the cooling cupcakes. "We have just enough cupcakes based on yesterday's sales," she stated before getting back on subject. "Not sure if banks can do much more for security. Half the time, I'm locked out of my online bank account because I capitalized the name of the city, I was born in."

"Um, you *are* supposed to capitalize proper nouns."

"Everybody knows that." Stephanie gave a huff of annoyance. "I was eating when I made up my password hints, so I typed with one hand, all lowercase. I tend to forget this and get locked out when I do online banking. Not sure if I can handle anything more complicated. Not sure where to start."

Della pursed her lips as she considered those whose accounts had been compromised. "Commonalities."

"Okay," Stephanie replied as she dropped dirty utensils into the sink, before adding, "What do we know about those who have been hit?"

"They're all female." Della shrugged her shoulders, and continued, "That means nothing since I interact with very few males. Maybe, they shop at the same store. All it takes is one unscrupulous employee. I'd better call Mother and tell her to look for contests and loyalty cards. People don't mind talking about their address or birthday, but when you start asking about loyalty cards, it gets weird." Della cleared her throat and corrected herself. "Gets *weirder.*"

Stephanie rolled her eyes. "It's bad when Uncle Wilbur suddenly becomes the voice of reason, even beyond the grave. I doubt he'd give out his birthday or phone number, either. Come to think of it, I don't think he had a phone. Didn't want people calling him up."

On cue, the bakery phone rang.

# CHAPTER NINETEEN

P HONE CALLS BEFORE opening usually meant demanding Bridezillas at the other end. Still, it could be someone who forgot the office goodies and needed Cupid's Catering to save the day. With that in mind, Della put an extra cheerfulness into her voice as she picked up the wall phone receiver. "Cupid's Catering Company. How can I help you?"

There was a breathy female on the other end. "Is this the owner? I need to speak to the owner."

Usually, requests such as that came with a complaint. Della would have known if something catastrophic had occurred at the bakery or a catering event. "This is Della Delacroix, the owner."

Her muscles tensed expecting some long-winded story about eating something at her bakery causing an allergic reaction. Soy, nuts, and corn syrup weren't used in her creations, and she had a limited number of gluten-free cookies she made with rice flour, but everyone should assume bakery goods were made with wheat flour, eggs, butter, and cane sugar along with various spices.

"You're my last hope!" the woman continued.

Ah, she nailed it the first time as a forgetful employee who slipped on ordering the meeting treats. "Glad I can help."

The unnamed woman continued, "I called Stuarts Done for You, Momma's Cooking, and Fleenor's Fine Foods, but they were no help."

The names belonged to local caterers, except for Fleenor's, which happened to be in Centerville. What could the woman want, especially at this early hour? "What type of assistance do you need?"

"Wedding. Small reception. I've made the food. By the way, this is Deborah Mifflin from Mifflin Catering."

Della recognized the name of Owens' premier caterer. When she decided to be a caterer, she never thought to compete against the likes of Mifflin Catering, who tended to handle the moneyed events and charge the most. Cupid's Catering was more for the everyday folks. The same people who might have a backyard wedding as opposed to renting out or owning a mansion. Mifflin handled the mansion set and those who wanted a big event. Why would Deborah call her?

At least her manners kicked in while her brain mulled over the reason behind the call. "I'm pleased to meet you."

She certainly posed no threat to Mifflin Catering and managed to survive the recent threat of her mean girl rival's Sweet Treasures. You'd think the universe would give her a pass on competitors, problems, or all of the above since her last encounter. Why couldn't caterers be more of associates as opposed to rivals?

"And me, you. I need someone to run the event for me. I received a call this morning that my father had a serious heart attack. Of course, I need to fly to Texas and stay with him. My usual assistant is on her honeymoon. This leaves me with no one to oversee the wedding. I have hourly employees, but no one who understands the organizational aspect. What I need is someone to run it. Did you understand the part about having all the food prepared?"

"I heard that. Sorry about your father." It would be the decent thing to help, but in the end, she'd only help her competitor look good. Her business sense battled with her kind nature. Maybe that was why the other caterers had turned her away. "I assume the other caterers were busy with their own events?"

"I don't know. They didn't say. Since you're mainly a bakery that closes early on Saturday, I thought you'd have the time."

Della held the phone from her ear and regarded it the same way she would an insect that showed up on her kitchen counter. A whole lot of assumptions existed in that statement. *Mainly a bakery* made it sound like the catering part of her business didn't matter. Then she made it sound like she had nothing to do on a Saturday night. Maybe she had a husband, kids, or even a dedicated date night. Of course, Deborah knew the general aspects of Della's life due to it being a small town. Her mother would share her marital status with everyone she encountered, hoping to hunt down possible son-in-law material.

The erasable marker calendar clung to the wall next to the phone. "When's your wedding?"

"This Saturday. I should be back by Monday. The last-minute favor is a great deal to expect."

Yes, it was. Part of her wanted to say yes, no matter what—the part of her that needed to be liked. She was reminded of the old story of two wolves—about the mother feeding the one she wanted to survive, which in her case tended to be positive business sense, and starving the other—people-pleasing. She made a decision.

"I could help, but what would be in it for me?"

"I'd pay you."

"That would make me just another employee."

A long pause sounded at the other end of the phone, until Deborah finally spoke, "What did you have in mind?"

Somehow, she needed to highlight the bakery, since drawing a spotlight on Cupid's Catering would not be something Deborah would agree to. "I could feature an item from the bakery at no cost to the client such as…" She paused as her eyes roamed over the items about to go out front. "…double chocolate cupcakes with a card denoting they were from Cupid's Catering Company."

"Hmm, I don't know. It seems counterproductive advertising another caterer at my event."

"Bakery. Who thinks cupcakes when it comes to caterers?"

"Good point."

"I'm your last hope."

A sigh carried over the phone. "That's true."

"Besides, if local businesses work together, we could accomplish more. We could host community events such as fun runs and the Mardi Gras next year."

"Mardi Gras? That sounds intriguing."

"And fun," Della made sure to add, knowing it would be a great deal of work, too. If Deborah signed on, others might follow suit. "We can talk about it when you come back."

"Can I consider that a yes?" An upward swing entered Deborah's voice.

"Well," Della hesitated, wanting to make sure Cupid's receive maximum benefit for her effort. "I get paid and get to feature some of my sweet treats along with proper signage."

"Signage?" Deborah's tone managed to convey both surprise and a certain reluctance.

"I did mention this earlier. How will people know I am the one behind the cupcakes?"

"You're welcome to tell people, but the sign might mislead people thinking you catered the whole thing. You can understand why that won't work for me."

"Fair enough." Della agreed, and it was more than she expected. As far as running around telling everyone she made the cupcakes, she couldn't see that happening. She'd have her hands full organizing the event. Still, if her mother attended, she'd be sure to get her name out there.

"Okay. When can we meet to go over the details?"

They pinned down a time the next day to discuss the event. Della picked up a marker and scribbled in the information on the calendar. *Riding to the rescue of another caterer.*

Stephanie grabbed a tray of cookies and backed into the swinging door. "I'm not sure how this can benefit us."

Inhaling deeply, Della debated if she'd done the right thing. Her goal included feeding the business sense wolf while starving the people-pleaser wolf, but she may have just fed both. "It will. I might be able to convince Deborah Mifflin to support the idea of a community Mardi Gras."

"Wow! Deborah Mifflin," Stephanie exclaimed and wrinkled her nose. "She has a reputation of not playing well with others."

Why had no one mentioned that important detail to Della before she made the deal?

# CHAPTER TWENTY

ONVERSATION AND LAUGHTER carried over from the café as Stephanie manned the counter with a little help from Elise, who managed to get permission to leave school early as part of a work shadow program. The upside for the hard-working senior was she'd get paid for her help, unlike the other shadowers who merely got experience and a reference. In the kitchen, foot-long buns were cut open, waiting to be loaded with meat and other toppings.

Della unwrapped the aromatic salami. "Do you think I should use this only with the Italian sub?"

Her mother, who stood on the other side of the island peeling divider wrappers off the provolone cheese, bobbed her head before speaking. "Definitely. It tends to overwhelm."

"That's what I thought." Della layered ten buns with the salami. Mabel followed with the provolone. Thinly sliced ham and *mortadella*, a top-shelf Italian version of bologna, finished off the sub. All condiments, along with lettuce, tomatoes, and pickles, would be offered on the side at a fixings bar. Sandwich creation became a bit of an assembly line since they had two hundred sandwiches to complete before delivering them to the center at four. Despite the rapid pace, they managed to converse.

Mabel wrapped up her sandwich and put a big *I* on it before inserting it into the box labeled *Italian subs*. "Heard much from

Guy?"

There was no need to ask what her mother meant since she saw the man once a week when she exchanged cookies for buns. "The usual. Also, he asked me to his cousin's wedding."

"A wedding!" Mabel cooed the words as she beamed. "How nice for you. You never know. You might catch the bouquet."

"I won't," Della affirmed, unwilling to be one of the women crowding around the bride, hoping that a chance-caught bouquet signaled an upcoming vows exchange. The bride usually hand-picks her catcher to assure the pricey bouquet could be saved as a wedding souvenir. "I refuse to huddle around the bride. My marital status doesn't depend on a superstition."

Her mother arched her eyebrows. "Something I need to know?"

"Nope. I'm sure with your gossip hotline, you'd know before I did."

Her mother smirked. "You're right about that. When's the cousin's wedding?"

"In about a month."

"Hmm," Mabel sniffed, and her eyes rolled upward as if trying to remember. "I don't know of any weddings happening in a month. Maybe you got the date wrong."

"Guy told me."

Mabel snorted. "Men. They aren't any good at dates. That's why they need women to keep them organized. You'd better ask again."

The normal response would be to tell her mother she didn't know every wedding happening in Owens, only she did. Clarice and Mabel crashed weddings but not for the usual free food and drink. They enjoyed the pageantry and the ceremonies. In some ways, it worked as live theatre. They sat in the back and crept out before the receiving line formed. Most people probably assumed they were distant cousins. Della could understand her mother's obsession with true love, but Clarice's attendance must count for gossip gathering only.

There was no way Della would ask Guy if he actually knew when his cousin's wedding was. Such an inquiry implied irresponsibility and poor time management skills. Sometimes, the best way to deal with troublesome questions was to change the subject. "Did you find out anything about your bank card not working?"

Her mother stopped in the middle of wrapping a sandwich. "Oh my, yes! Should have mentioned it when I came in. I talked to the bank manager, Frank. We attended school together. Due to a late birthday, he was only a junior when I graduated. Anyhow, he commented on how I wasn't the only one to have issues with my bank card. He acted baffled, but not alarmed. Called it a digital failure, but they had redundancy in the network that caused any suspect accounts to freeze."

That much had been obvious. "Why was your account suspect?"

"Talk about weird." Mabel's gaze slipped down to her hands that rested motionless on the counter. "Good heavens, I'm not multi-tasking very well." She started wrapping sandwiches again and forgot to finish her statement.

"What's weird?" Della prompted, aware her mother was acting rattled, which for the unflappable female, rang alarm bells.

"The bank manager said the access log stated someone tried to access my account multiple times."

Identity thieves broke into accounts using the actual owner's birthdate and had about a fifty percent chance of being right. "This is what you thought happened. Did you lose a bank card recently?

Maybe put in the wrong number?"

"No." Mabel inhaled deeply, although her face paled. "I have one bank card, which I'm in possession of. My password is the model of my first car. Only one person knows this."

"Clarice?" Della guessed.

"No, your father," Mabel continued somberly. "I think your father is trying to communicate with me."

A fair number of reality shows featured ghost hunters who swore ghosts manipulated electronics and electricity. They could turn appliances and lights off and on. Some could even leave messages on answering machines or tap out a note on a laptop. Unfortunately for the reality shows' ratings, none ever chose to do that while the cameras were running. Most ghosts tended to be camera shy and left their messages after the cameras shut down for the day. As far as Della could remember, none used ATMs.

"What's he trying to say?"

"Probably *don't spend so much*. You remember how frugal he was."

While no one had ever accused her father of wasting money, the same could also be said about her mother. "Why now? He had seven years to do something."

"Time moves differently on the other side. How else can you explain my bank account being tampered with internally?"

"Internally. Like inside the machine? That makes no sense at all. How could that happen?"

"It's Kenneth, I tell you."

It was not an answer Della bought. "What if it was someone who loaded the machine or programed it or something?"

Color pinked Mabel's cheeks as she pressed her hands together in front of her. "You mean it's probably *not* Kenneth blocking my access to money after buying those winter boots at full price?"

"Mom, be serious. Dad bought you a car with all the bells and whistles. I doubt he'd begrudge you a pair of snow boots."

"Good to know." She wrapped a few more sandwiches before her head snapped up and met her daughter's gaze. "That means someone could be messing with the ATMs and the bank accounts. An inside job."

"My thoughts exactly."

A slap on the back door and an outside bark clued the sandwich makers something was up. The door swung open, and Tony, the dog, rushed in, trailed by a bruised Lorna holding the leash. Della leaned forward, spreading her arms wide and trying to cover the sandwiches in progress. "You can't have a dog in here!"

Her mother's head went up. "My Tony's a clean dog."

"Board of Health would shut me down in a minute, no matter how clean your pet is."

Lorna started backing out with the dog, apologizing as she went. "Sorry. Something happened I thought you needed to know about. When I received a call from Bookmania, I just panicked. Suddenly, I didn't feel safe anymore."

Lorna stepped out but left the door open to converse. They'd have to go outside or risk being overheard. Both Della and Mabel hurried into the cold to discover what had forced Lorna out of her safe sanctuary. Their sudden exit had them chafing their bare arms and awkwardly dancing to stay warm.

Della took two sliding steps, then stomped her feet. "What did Bookmania say?"

"They asked me about my upcoming signing on my newest

release." Lorna fiddled with the leash as she spoke, wrapping it around one hand, releasing it, and then starting the entire procedure over again.

Obviously, the reluctant author needed some time before appearing in public. "You could postpone the signing."

"That's just it. I didn't make the appointment. Bookmania called to ask me what books I wanted pulled for signing."

"Oh." The puzzle pieces began to come together. Breaking into Lorna's abode to steal her vocation rated as extremely foolhardy. Holding a book signing in the author's hometown had to be icing on top of the stupid cake. "What did you tell Bookmania?"

"I'd call them back."

"That was smart of you. As hard as it is for me to believe, it sounds like your attackers are going for a book signing. Makes me wonder which one is going to dress up as you. Call Bookmania and give them some titles to pull. We're going to have to stop by the station and talk to the police."

Lorna grimaced. "I hope I don't get that rude detective again."

"No worries." Mabel waved her hand back and forth as if clearing away a bad memory or possibly trying to stay warm. "I've already talked to Delores about it, who in turn talked to Weathered Leather."

"Who? What?" Lorna questioned, and Tony gave a sharp bark, adding his opinion or perhaps expressing his discontent about the cold.

Mabel pointed to Lorna's car. "Get my dog home and you, too. Don't worry about the book signing. We'll work it out. I'll give you a call when to come to the station" She gave a heavy sigh. "Looks like I'll need to play nice with the commissioner."

# CHAPTER TWENTY-ONE

THE POSSIBILITY OF Lorna's home invaders returning made her reluctant to go back to Mabel's empty house even with the ever-vocal Tony. Fortunately, Vanessa's house—next-door to Mabel's—was outfitted more like Fort Knox since her own run-in with thieves. It served as her new sanctuary, complete with the hostess, Vanessa, sharing her favorite game shows.

A little past five Mabel and Della arrived, followed shortly by a sedan, complete with numerous antennas.

Della slammed the car door and headed to the side entrance, while Mabel waited for the commissioner to exit his vehicle. The two of them walked to the entrance while Della shamelessly eavesdropped.

Mabel flashed a sincere, wide smile as she spoke. "It's nice of you to come out and meet with Lorna."

The man coughed and then cleared his throat and managed a grave, "I think I should, considering."

Not exactly an apology for the high-handed treatment Lorna had received from a certain police detective, but it might be a bit of damage control before things got worse. Who knows what else the bold attackers might try? Big City Detective probably thought crime never visited Owens, which could explain why he moved here.

Della balled up her hand and knocked.

Vanessa called from the other side, "What's the password?"

Password? They hadn't discussed any password. She cut her eyes to her mother, who shrugged. Great. Knowing Vanessa, she'd refuse to answer the door despite being able to see them on the doorbell camera. Unable to think of a clever word or phrase, Della said, "Password?"

The door opened a crack with Vanessa sticking her face in the opening. "You got it in one. Good girl." She grinned at Della and then pointed behind her. "Who's the man?"

"Police Commissioner Edward Jennings," the man in question articulated as he pushed his shoulders back and sucked in his stomach. He waited for recognition or possibly awe but received neither.

"Show me some identification," Vanessa demanded in a no-nonsense tone. "I didn't fall off a turnip truck. Plenty of folks have been fooled by a title or even fraudulent documents." She cocked her head in Mabel's direction. "Surely you asked for some ID, especially after the movie of the week about the woman giving vital information to the man, she thought was a detective but was actually trying to track down her husband to hurt him."

Mabel remained silent.

Even though her mother's neighbor usually set her dial to outrageous, this time she made sense. How did they know this man headed up the police department? He could have fooled the entire department. After all, Owens never had a commissioner before. Della watched Edward Jennings out of the corner of her eye as he reached for his back pocket, extracted a leather wallet, and flipped it open. A badge glinted before he closed the cover and returned it to his pocket.

"Not so fast!" Vanessa shot out her hand. "I need to see it in good light."

Once the badge hit her hand, Vanessa wrapped her fingers around it, withdrew, and slammed the door. The unexpected action had Della shaking her head, while her mother pressed her lips together to stifle a giggle.

A hearty laugh erupted from the commissioner, who slapped his leg. "Good call. All citizens should demand ID. I imagine she's either calling the police department or looking me up on the Internet."

"Probably both," Mabel added and then giggled. "I will say Vanessa has more reason than most to be careful."

A few minutes later, the door swung open. Vanessa motioned them to come in. "Everything checks out. I'm not worried about myself. Probably could take you with an oversized mag light and a can of wasp spray. I may be old, but I'm feisty." She handed the badge back to Jennings. "I need to watch out for my cat, Tunameister, and my guest." She nodded in Mabel's direction and added, "And, of course, your prissy dog, Tony."

"Hey!" Mabel objected. "Tony's not prissy."

"You bought him rainboots and a raincoat," Vanessa announced with a smirk.

Geesh, here Della thought her mother and Vanessa had made up after their last case, but they were both grinning. Some habits people must just hold onto despite the lack of need for sniping.

The two friends bickered back and forth about inconsequential things, with the commissioner trying to get a handle on the conversation without any luck. "Ladies," he uttered a half-dozen times.

Not needing to say anything, Della knew they'd wind down on

their own. In some ways, it served as their greeting, the way some people hugged.

Lorna wandered into the room, carrying the Himalayan cat. "I thought I heard knocking."

Della noted she said nothing about two women arguing, which had to be louder and more annoying than the knocking. Both women stopped on cue and turned toward Lorna, inquiring about her well-being at the same time.

The commissioner settled for clearing his throat just as another knock sounded. "That must be Detective Ramirez. Just made detective, but he's sharp. I asked him to sit in on the meeting."

Vanessa cracked the door, peeked out, and swung the door wide to allow entry for the handsome, thirty-something detective. Ruffled by this deviation from her normal routine, the commissioner asked, "Why didn't you ask for *his* identification?"

Vanessa blinked once and turned a blank face to her questioner. "He looks honest. You, on the other hand..." She left the statement unfinished.

THE SIX OF them searched for seats, which meant uncovering a loveseat draped with blankets and throw pillows, moving a Raggedy Andy doll from a rocking chair, and encouraging Tony to abandon the sofa. Vanessa ducked into the next room to pull kitchen chairs into duty.

Once they had a rough circle, the commissioner nodded in Lorna's direction. "I apologize for making you retell your ordeal, but Detective Ramirez needs to be brought up to speed on your case. He'll be the detective you'll be working with from now on."

A heavy exhale came from Lorna, indicating she may have been holding her breath. "Thank you," she whispered. Her voice gained strength as she explained what happened. Anger punctuated her narrative as she explained being left for dead.

The detective raised one finger. "The attackers think you're dead?"

"Yes," Lorna answered and bobbed her head. "They didn't stick around to check if I was still moving. The fact they contacted the bookstore to do a book signing pretty much says it all. They had no clue the store would call me about which books to pull."

Detective Ramirez narrowed his eyes and stroked his chin. "No news reports. Obituaries, etc."

Masculine throat-clearing drew their eyes to the commissioner. The throat clearing probably functioned as his attention-getting device rather like a herald yelling, *Get ready. The big guy is going to speak.*

All faces turned toward him. "I killed the story. It wasn't hard since your initial detective never reported it to the crime beat reporter." He ducked his head and then continued, "You know why."

Lorna had no such qualms about stating why. She held up her head and stared back at the man. "The initial detective who took my report thought I battered myself with a tire iron, wrecked my house, and alarmed my neighbors in an effort to gain publicity."

"Yeah, that," the commissioner continued and arched one eyebrow. "As reprehensible as that seems now, it works in our favor. The thugs believe they got away with it."

A tutting sound expressed Vanessa's disbelief, which she was willing to elaborate on. "Wouldn't they read the newspapers? Look for an obituary?"

Before the commissioner could answer, Mabel did. "They don't sound like members of the brain trust. Also, it takes a while to plan a funeral. The family could also decide to keep it private, which would make sense for a crime victim. No need to make it a public spectacle."

"All good reasons," the commissioner agreed. "My thoughts are along the lines that perps concentrate on the crime, not the consequences. You'd be surprised how many are genuinely surprised when they're arrested." He shook his head as if the concept baffled him. "A few even explained to me why they shouldn't be arrested for the perfect crime they'd orchestrated."

A silence descended upon the room with the exception of muffled game show contestants. A few may have waited for anything else the big guy might say, but most of the room's attention shifted to Tony, who cautiously approached Tunameister. The cat swished his sizable tail as a warning. All the same, the Italian Greyhound continued his curious inspection. About the time Della expected the cat to leap into action and give the dog a claw-laden swipe for his effrontery, the long pup nose touched the flat cat nose and a communal "ah" sounded from the humans. Satisfied with the reception, Tony settled down next to Tunameister to sleep.

Ramirez gauged the room and then nodded at Lorna. "I understood the perps called the local bookstore for a signing?"

"The nerve of them!" Vanessa popped up from her seat and threw up her hands. "Do they think local readers are fools?"

"They must," Lorna said and smiled in Vanessa's direction. "I appreciate your outrage on my behalf and on behalf of my readers. Not sure what they expect from the signing. Boatloads of money?"

"What type of money could you expect from a signing?"

Ramirez asked and pulled out a tablet and a pen. "I tend to be old school about notes."

"No problem." Lorna's eyes flickered upward. "It depends on the signing. I usually limit it to two hundred presale tickets. That usually runs between three and four hours depending on if the readers want photos. With the bookstore, the agent, and the publisher taking their cuts, I could make around six hundred dollars if everyone buys one hardback book. Many bring books they have bought previously or have been gifted. Others buying two or more books helps my bottom line."

The pen racing across the paper combined with the snores of sleeping animals served as an audio backdrop. Ramirez glanced up. "It doesn't sound like boatloads of money."

"Far from it. I count myself lucky to make a living. I assume my attackers pulled my address from one of my newsletters. A writer friend kept urging me to get a P.O. Box." Her shoulders went up in a shrug. "I told her I live in small-town America. Nothing to worry about. I should have listened."

She stumbled to a halt and murmured something under her breath that sounded a lot like *fools*. "Anyone driving into my neighborhood should have noticed the lack of expensive vehicles, acres of manicured lawns, and a fleet of gardeners keeping them that way. Nope, they barged straight on with a plan that had to be hatched over a bottle of bottom-shelf whiskey."

"You're probably right about how the plan came about," Ramirez said and wrote down a few more notes. "So far, nothing has happened to them, and they assume their plan to become you is going full steam. Does the bookstore pay you on the day of the signing?"

"Sometimes. They usually cut me a check written to my legal name. I'm not certain how they'd cash that."

"Unfortunately, there are a few unscrupulous cash checking places squatting on the county line that have been fined more than once for accepting stolen checks, but they ask such a high percentage to cash a check that only the most desperate use their services. There's a good chance our would-be authors would head there. Our goal is to catch them at the book signing. Would you recognize the men?"

"Absolutely." Lorna spoke with conviction as her hands balled into fists. Then she exhaled hard and spoke in a wavering voice. "But they'll recognize me."

"You'll need a disguise," Mabel volunteered.

Della thought she knew what her mother might suggest. "Not the clown outfit. It would stand out at a book signing."

Her mother gave a derisive snort and then told Lorna, "I happen to know a makeup artist. She even worked in Hollywood. Your own mother wouldn't recognize you."

"Sounds like a plan," Ramirez offered and then scribbled something else on his pad. "I'll need to contact the bookstore manager. We'll have to have them on board when someone shows up who is clearly not you. We'll need fans, too. I don't want to put citizens at risk." His brow wrinkled as he pondered the situation.

"How about our newest class of recruits at the police academy?" the commissioner suggested, which made it pretty much a done deal. "It would be their first undercover assignment. Great training."

"That could work. I'll need to tell the recruits what their cover is and how they should dress. What type of books do you write?"

"Romance," Lorna said with a straight face, which was better than Della could do imagining all the young, clean-faced recruits, some with military hairstyles, standing in line, clutching Lorna's latest romance with an embracing couple emblazoned across the front.

"That could be problematic."

"You'd be surprised who reads romance. Many men do. It's not just women."

"Got it." He gave her a thumbs up, closed his tablet, and pulled a business card from his wallet which he handed to Lorna. "Give me a call if anything else comes up before Friday."

The commissioner took this as his cue to leave and bid the women goodbye. Mabel waited for the door to close before addressing her friend. "Why didn't you check Ramirez's ID?"

"Mercy!" Vanessa sniffed. "Surely you recognized Maria's son."

"You're right." Mabel made a face as if it pained her to admit it but continued gamely, "He looks more like his father. You really burned the commissioner by refusing to check Ramirez's ID."

"I know it," Vanessa acknowledged with a grin. "The man needs to be taken down a peg or two, and I'm just the person to do it. Where did he come from?"

"I don't know. Not from here. I'd better call Melanie, the makeup artist. Plenty of women will be wanting to be made up for winter weddings or the Police Ball. I need to get in before she's booked."

Shouldn't an actual crime take precedence over a fancy dance? "Mom, why don't you tell her it's for a case?"

Her mother held a finger up to her lips. "The more people know, the bigger the chance the perps will find out, too. Don't worry, we'll come up with an excuse."

# CHAPTER TWENTY-TWO

S TAKING OUT A bookstore to see who might be impersonating Lorna didn't fit into Della's schedule, but her mother felt they should show for moral support. They arrived with a copy of the latest release for fake Lorna to sign. While the cover intrigued Della, she'd tear out the page if the faker signed it.

In an effort not to attract attention, they all wore hats to shade their faces from recognition. Vanessa went in first with a droopy garden party number that must have been from a 1970s wedding. Her mother took advantage of one of the fedoras she'd bought her husband. Normally, Della avoided hats, having a big head that resulted in her hair ballooning out around the hat rim. It's not a good look on her or anyone. Someone had given her a black beanie with *I Have Issues* printed on it. She couldn't remember who. Pulling it down to her brows contained her wayward hair and made her less recognizable.

When she entered and paused to riffle through a table of clearance items, Della mentally congratulated herself on slipping in unnoticed, that is, until she saw Ramirez looking decidedly embarrassed while sporting a purple shirt announcing *Romance Rocks My Boat*. An image of a boat with only a pair of feet showing above the side of the craft covered the front. He grumbled about too many citizens getting in the way of the experts. His gaze stopped on Della, and then over to the biographies where Mabel and Vanessa stood.

They might have been swept out the door if the bookstore manager hadn't spotted them. The thin, nervous woman, mistaking them for actual customers, herded the three of them back to the romance section of the bookstore, mentioning something about a must-see new release. Her attitude probably had more to do with keeping them out of the line of fire.

Bookstores seldom raked in the money, especially on books alone, which accounted for the addition of music, stationery, games, and even toys pertinent to popular series. The scent of cinnamon and freshly brewed coffee hung in the air, reminding Della of the pocket-sized coffee shop in the upper left corner of the store. How many employees were in the store? An almost empty store with a handful of ill-chosen romance fans might spook Lorna's attackers. Then again, they had no clue what constituted a romance fan.

The bell above the entrance rang as a woman with dark, black hair and a face made up like Cleopatra entered. Her mother muttered something under her breath.

Della, unsure if her remark had been intended for all, said, "Pardon me?"

"The makeup artist I got for Lorna did work in Hollywood, but I forgot she only got to work on one movie set."

That explained it. "Let me guess, an ancient Egyptian saga?"

"Yep. She has two modes: bridal and apparently, ancient Egyptian. Lorna probably told her not to do bridal because she didn't want to stand out."

Vanessa rocked to her tiptoes to get a better look. "Well, the not standing out might be difficult. She reminds me of one of those silver screen silent picture actresses. Not that I've seen any silent pictures, but I've seen photos from those Hollywood insider type of books."

The bookstore manager moved from behind the shelves to have a view not impaired by shelves or people. "If you hadn't said anything, I'd never have known it was Lorna. How can you be sure? Some of the fans really doll themselves up for the photoshoot, knowing they'll have a photo with the author. A few try to dress as a character from the book." She paused and held a finger to her lips before continuing. "It's been forever since Lorna wrote period romance, but I do recall something about a pharaoh. It could be a fan demonstrating her memory and devotion."

The last thing they needed was another Lorna, only this one would be disguised as an Egyptian princess. If Lorna and Della had been tight friends, she could have picked her out by the way she walked. The made-up woman gazed around and then took a few hesitant steps, appearing unaware of what to do. Della waved, making an arc above the bookshelves. She refrained from yelling, not wanting to attract Detective Ramirez's attention.

Spotting them, Lorna hurried over to the group or as well as she could in her platform shoes. Once there, she grabbed onto a bookshelf to steady herself. "I thought platforms went out in the 1980s."

"Me, too," Della agreed. "Why are you wearing them? They look painful."

"They are." She winced as she made her way over to an over-stuffed chair meant to tempt the potential book buyer to read one more page. She collapsed into the chair with a sigh. "The detective thought it would make me a different height and less recognizable. As for the shoes, they came from the police's undercover wardrobe closet, and they are a smidge too small. Probably more than a smidge."

"Hmm," Mabel murmured as she gave the platform shoes a close inspection. "My husband never talked much about undercover work. However, at the time those shoes were worn, he might not have been on the force. I can't imagine Kenneth wearing them." She chuckled, which caused a woman to hurry over to them.

The blonde woman had scads of perfect corkscrew curls that fell to her waist and sported a shirt covered with hearts and painted on jeggings. She held one finger up. "Ladies, it's fine to talk, but keep it down. Remember, this is a bookstore." She pointed to Lorna. "You're with me."

"Do I have to? No one is here, and these shoes are murder."

The woman glanced back over her shoulder. "Okay. I see your point. Stay here and I'll get you when needed."

Before the undercover officer left, Vanessa asked, "Your hair. It's a wig, right?"

"Seriously? That's your question?" She strode off without answering.

Vanessa sniffed and then declared, "It's definitely a wig."

"You have to wonder what exactly they're doing with their undercover wardrobe. I thought Owens to be small-town safe," Mabel mused and frowned.

"You'd be surprised." The bookstore manager gestured to the true-crime fiction area behind the romance shelves. "Plenty of serial killings happened in small towns. I have the books to prove it."

From her spot on the comfy chair, Lorna sighed. "That does absolutely nothing to reassure me."

"Not you, dear. Not Owens. Other places, not here," the store manager rambled in her attempt to reassure.

Ramirez made his way to the group and gave a sharp nod in the bookstore manager's direction. "I need you up front." He raised his fingers to make air quotes. "When Lorna walks in, you'll need to be near the entrance to welcome and guide her to the table. This is your chance of a lifetime acting opportunity."

"I've never wanted to act." The store manager's voice shook.

"You agreed to do this. We can't put one of our officers in your place because the suspects may know who runs the store."

"Do it for me," Lorna begged and then added with a smile, "In my next book, I'll name my main character after you."

"Winnifred?" She placed a hand against her chest and beamed.

"Maybe just Winnie, since I'm writing contemporaries."

The manager squared her shoulders, lifted her chin, and spoke in a confident, strong voice. "I'm ready, or should I say, *Winnie* is ready."

If Ramirez rolled his eyes at the transformation, Della didn't see it. The four of them entertained themselves by picking up various books and describing the plots by either the title or the cover. Other people arrived. Della turned and scanned each newcomer, trying to decide if they were undercover or a simple book buyer. Perhaps not many buyers would come today. Hardcore readers would want to stock up for the weekend, though.

Four women grouped together wouldn't look natural, since most readers searched on their own and not in a pack. Vanessa moved to a different shelf to see better. Mabel made her way to the true-crime section to make sure no nearby towns were featured in the books.

Not wanting to attract attention, Della sat on the floor next to Lorna's chair and whispered, "This will be over soon."

"I certainly hope so. Talk about a nightmare that will not end. I'm not sure why anyone would want to be me even if they could write. It's far from the glamorous life."

"Hard to say. Just recently I had a high school nemesis decide she wanted to run a bakery. All I can say is you really have to *love* baking to want to do that. I'm sure it's the same with writing."

"Yeah," Lorna spoke but then lapsed into silence. "I remember her. Fortunately, I was neither attractive nor popular enough to attract her attention."

They sat, not speaking until Corkscrew Blonde returned. "They're here. I need you. They found an actual female to impersonate you, but the two guys are hanging around the table. All I need you to do is a simple identification."

"Okay." Lorna inhaled deeply and pushed herself out of the chair. No one told Della she couldn't come. She waited until they were almost ten feet away before making her move. She grabbed the book to be signed at the last moment.

At the edge of the crowd, she met her mother and Vanessa, who hissed, "Look at that horrible wig. It's worse than the corkscrew wig. They must have bought it at the Halloween store. Cheap."

"Shush," her mother implored, but stared straight ahead at the dumpy woman with the before mentioned cheap, blond wig. It had a flat spot as if it had been resting on a shelf for a while. Bright red lipstick and oversized hoop earrings completed the disguise. Hadn't they even turned over her book to look at the author photo? Lorna would never dress like that.

The imposters settled into the roles of demanding author and cronies by insisting on specialty coffees that the bookstore manager retrieved for them. Not familiar with the signing protocol, they allowed the bookstore manager to give a little speech beforehand about each patron having up to two books signed, but no more, and while they could talk to the author, they could not engage her in long conversations about characters, plot lines, or motivations.

She stepped to the side as the blonde in the bad wig laced her fingers together and turned her hands outward, cracking her knuckles. After that, she followed up with banging on the table with a fisted hand and announced, "Let's get this party started."

The first officer, a grizzled-looking man in a newsboy cap came forward, grinning as he handed off his book to be signed. "Sign it to Edgar, you're my inspiration, my star, my…"

The taller man hovering near the table stepped menacingly toward the autograph seeker. "You're not getting a book written about you. Be satisfied with what you get and get lost."

Flashes went off as several snapshots were taken.

"What was that?" the tall thug demanded.

The pretend author simpered. "It's my adoring fans. Of course they'd want a photo of me." She signed another book with a flourish and handed it back to a middle-aged woman who resembled the police dispatcher.

The shorter thug scissored his arms, forming an X as he announced, "No photos today. They cost extra. Hundred dollars. Got an extra hundred? Come see me. We can arrange something."

"Spoken like a true con artist." Her mother muttered the words loud enough for Della to hear and possibly a few other folks.

One woman shushed her. A soft patter of voices continued as fans shuffled up to the table, spoke a few words, and received their fraudulently signed books. A low conversation started near Della's left before she could locate the talkers.

Lorna's voice rang out. "That's them!" She pointed straight at the men as if there was any question. "Those are the men who tried to kill me and steal my writer's reputation!"

The signing woman jerked sharply as if shot and then snarled at the taller man. "You told me she was dead! This was supposed to be *my* time to be a star!"

Clearance table books tumbled over as one thug darted for the door, pushing his way through eager fans. Lorna dropped to the floor, taking cover behind a cardboard promotion trumpeting the joys of winter romance.

Spotting the second thug heading toward the coffee shop and possibly an exterior door sent Vanessa into high alert screaming, "He's getting away! Someone do something!

Della didn't know who someone was supposed to be. Didn't they heavily salt the fans with undercover cops? Uncertain what to do, she dashed into the tiny coffee shop, grabbed a heavy saucepan possibly used for hot chocolate and aimed it at the escaping man. It went high, bounced off the wall, and ricocheted into the man, causing him to stumble mid-stride. He turned slowly to view whoever threw the pan. Della dropped to her knees behind a box of individually wrapped sugar cookies, knowing if the man had a gun, the cardboard, cellophane, and questionable cookies would do little to save her. Time slowed down as her heartbeat raced and she reminded herself she didn't have what it took to be an action hero.

A shout sounded from the other side of the coffee shop as a uniformed officer came through the exterior door and ordered the man to freeze. Not one to take orders, he darted for the front door, but Corkscrew Blonde tackled him from behind. Della stood slowly and blinked. Where had she come from? It didn't matter, only that she showed up when she did.

Her heart managed to slow to a reasonable rate as several "fans" worked their way behind the suspects, quietly handcuffing and escorting the two men out of the building.

Fake Lorna had stayed frozen behind the table as the chase ensued. With both men captured, she must have assumed she'd be next. Her hands gripped the table and pushed it over, sending coffee and books flying. A few devoted fans dove for the books before the hazelnut coffee stained the pages. The woman feinted in the direction of the coffee shop but ended up running to the back of the store. Ironically, an officer nabbed her in the true crime section.

Her wig slipped off, revealing a wig cap and flattened gray hair underneath. As the officers moved her out of the building, the woman offered her excuses. "This was a present from my son. You see, I always wanted to be a writer but never really got the chance. It's hard to break into the business."

Della never heard the end of the excuse, but she doubted any judge would be sympathetic. For all she knew, the mother could be the mastermind behind everything.

Lorna moved toward the now righted table with haphazardly stacked books and held up her hands for attention. "If any of you are actual fans and want your books signed, I'll be happy to do it. Make sure to look for my next book because I wouldn't be surprised if the truth behind this escapade plays a major part of the plot."

Her mother nudged Della. "Looks like this part of our mystery is solved, but now we have monetary issues to solve."

True enough. There still was the issue with the vanishing money, but a spark of an idea formed. "You remember how frustrated you'd get about not being able to balance your checking account?"

"Do I ever, but it's never enough to break me. Maybe fifty cents, a dollar. One time, it was five dollars. I convinced myself someone never cashed a check on that one."

The wheels were starting to turn. "Find out if others are having the same issues. I'm trying out a theory. In the meantime, I'm staying here to support Lorna. I imagine she's still a little shaky despite the baddies being rounded up and driven away."

# CHAPTER TWENTY-THREE

THE BOOKSTORE MANAGER must have hit social media about a surprise signing. After fraudulent Lorna left, cuffed and stuffed into a squad car, women arrived in groups of twos and fours as if someone had careened around the neighborhood, yelling through an open car window, "Surprise book signing!" It wasn't exactly "the British are coming," but it did get folks into the store. A few arrived in scrubs and another one wore a chain restaurant uniform.

When Vanessa and her mother left, Della assumed she'd follow with Lorna in ten minutes or so—not so much when the crowd arrived. She pulled out her phone and sent a text to Stephanie. Fortunately, the fake signing occurred after the lunch rush, and her high school helper would be in to help soon. Normally, Fridays didn't rate as her busy time, but today she needed to get back to the bakery and frost her double chocolate cupcakes for tomorrow's wedding reception.

Lorna ripped off the black wig and fluffed up her hair before she sat down to sign. There was not much she could do about her makeup. Half of her fans complimented it. Not knowing what to do, Della hovered nearby, handing off markers, tissues, or cough drops when asked. This must be what it would be like to be an assistant to a famous person—pretty boring, but it gave her time to think about the missing money.

From what she gathered, the problems stemmed from bank accounts not having funds or ATM cards not working. On the surface, it could be identity theft. An anonymous person could be filling out applications using someone else's name and address along with their credit history. If the new credit card had gone to a regular address, the mail could be forwarded by filling out a form online. Even though credit cards had a warning stamped on the envelope in about a 9-point, bold font that instructed *do not forward*, some probably were. She'd heard of people checking mailboxes for possible credit cards, which stunned her. Such a high chance of getting caught and very little possibility of succeeding seemed a waste of time. So far, no one complained about people casing their mailboxes or getting bills for credit cards they didn't have.

The squeak of a metal cart broke into her reverie. The store manager, recognizing a sales situation, pushed a cart with probably every Lorna book the store owned. "Look what I found! Some exclusive buys from the backlist."

There was no need to mention they could get the same books cheaper online. What they couldn't get was them being signed by the author and a couple of minutes to chat with Lorna. It took less than five minutes for the books to vanish. The manager crossed her arms and stood beside Della, keeping an eagle eye on the hands clutching unpaid for books. "Normally, I make them pay for the book before having it signed. Nothing's been normal today. If someone discovers they don't have the money to pay for a signed book, I guess I can resell it or offer a layaway plan if it's been personalized."

Della half-listened, still trying to form a theory about the missing funds. "How many banks does Owens have?"

"You mean branches or actual banks?"

"Actual banks." Della waited for an answer while wiggling a tissue to entertain a baby in a stroller until her mother finished getting her book signed.

"Three. No, four. A new bank with the sun coming up over the horizon logo put a branch in at Jiffy Foods."

That wouldn't be a contender. How many accounts could that little branch have? She needed something bigger. A memory about a book she read—maybe it was a movie—pushed its way into the front of her thoughts. Somehow, an employee in the bank would slowly siphon money to a fraudulent account. It was never a lot, and sometimes when people got suspicious, money was moved again from another account that was seldom accessed, such as savings accounts. Her mouth twisted to one side as she tried to remember how it happened. Had they even explained it or cautiously didn't, convinced it might cause a copycat crime?

Once the baby left, Della wadded up the tissue and put it into her pocket. "What's the biggest bank?"

"Owens Fidelity." The manager continued to wave fans in the direction of the cash register line just in case someone, in their excitement about a signed book, made the mistake of walking out without paying. She turned back to continue the conversation. "For the longest time, it was the only bank in Owens."

Bingo. Just what she needed. "How long was it the only bank?"

"About forever." The manager's brow furrowed as she gave it some thought. "I think the second bank showed up about five years ago. Union Bank. I've considered switching. The fees are so high on credit cards at Fidelity, plus I swear I keep losing money on my account. Nothing big, five dollars here, ten there, but it all adds up, especially over a year. Still, it takes forever to change banks, especially with a business. They have you fill out all these surveys and act hurt that you want to leave. Despite it being your money, you end up paying a fee to close the account."

It sounded normal. There had to be some way to make up for all the service fees they'd lose. It served as one more brick in her theory. Her father enjoyed a show that featured a cigar-chomping guy that always mentioned how he loved it when a plan came together. Della loved it, too. A few more bricks and she'd confirm her theory.

"You have an account at Owens Fidelity for very long?"

"For the last twenty years. You know something?"

She waved away the question, not wanting to cause panic, especially if no reason existed. Doing so would get her into hot water and possibly sued. "Nope. I'm a Union Bank person."

"Uh-huh." Her tone sounded far from convinced. "Let me know if you do hear something. We local businesspeople need to stick together."

"Will do." The iconic light bulb just switched on "Have you heard about the Mardi Gras or our town's take on it?"

Having another person to sell on the Mardi Gras idea, the two conversed until Lorna signed her last book. After thanking everyone, the author shouldered her purse and followed Della out, leaving the wig behind.

In the car, Della asked the all-important question, "Where should I drop you off?"

"Maybe I should go back to my house."

The car sputtered to life, but Della had no clue where to head. "Would you like to keep staying with my mother?"

"Do you think she'd let me?" Hope flavored her tone.

"Sure. She'd tell you to stay as long as you please. I'm not even sure if the forensic team is done with your house."

What she didn't say was she didn't know if a forensic team had even *visited* the house. Sure, they'd bumped into the commissioner on their own informal visit, but he and an officer didn't equate to a CSI team. Still, now that they'd rounded up the culprits, they'd need more evidence to solidify the case.

Della reversed the vehicle and headed toward her mother's house. Even though she and Lorna had been friends in high school, they'd lost touch, which gave them very little to talk about besides the home invaders.

Why not tackle the elephant in the room? "I guess it's hard for you to feel safe going back to your old place?"

"You got that right." She spat out the words and sighed. "I don't know if I will ever go back. My landlady came by the hospital and told me if I wanted to move, she wouldn't contest it. I think she was really saying *move because I can't deal with another break-in. It makes the other renters nervous.* Don't know where I'm going to relocate, but I have to agree with my landlady that moving will be the best choice."

Della mulled over the words as she waited at the stoplight. While her apartment building was far from primo, she knew feeling unsafe didn't allow a tenant to break a lease. Being a victim of a crime was another matter, especially if the tenant could prove the landlord was negligent. Those two glass panels by the door made entry simple. No wonder the landlady urged moving before Lorna concentrated too hard on her condo's security or lack of it.

"I can't recommend where *I* live. They don't keep it up, but on the other hand, it's cheap, which serves my purposes."

"I hear you on that. I'd love for this story not to make the papers, but since there is little newsworthy in Owens besides Scoutorama, the historical home tour, or the quarter-mile long yard sale, I imagine this will end up in the paper and possibly spun into a tale different from what actually happened. Folks will come by for a look-see after church. Yeah, I could do without all that. Even worse, what about those who think they could do something similar, a copycat crime?"

Her father was never a fan of true crime shows explaining to those with no scruples how to commit a crime they hadn't considered until they saw the show.

"I understand your fears. I'm sure Mom will let you stay as long as you need to and when you're ready, I'll help you move."

"Pretty decent of you." Lorna chuckled, albeit weakly. "That describes your whole family—decent. Of course, when I called from the hospital, I didn't know your dad had passed, but you and your mother have done him proud. Everything I hoped would happen due to your father's assistance happened anyhow."

"Thanks." Della swallowed as emotion choked her, and she did her best not to cry. One solitary tear slipped down her cheek. Making her father proud was high praise indeed. Silence settled over the two of them, each being caught in her own thoughts. The music from the radio washed over them—something about sailing. Her mouth quirked up into a smirk. Those living in the Midwest struggling through the winter would probably hate the sentiment, imagining happier, warmer folks on a sunset cruise. Others might get online and start planning their own tropical getaway. The idea tempted her, but outstanding duties, including an unsolved financial mystery, made it just a dream at this point.

# CHAPTER TWENTY-FOUR

AFTER THE EXCITEMENT of the afternoon, arriving at the bakery served as a reprieve. With only half an hour before closing, only a few customers waited in line to take advantage of their daily special. Stephanie handed over filled boxes of cookies with a smile. She waited until the bell jingled, announcing the last customer had exited before addressing Della.

"I know it's been a hard day, but you're officially out of cookies."

Della's eyebrows shot up. "Really? Not sure if that's ever happened before."

"It has now, which means you're going to have to make more for tomorrow."

"Goes without saying." She retrieved her phone from her purse, glanced at it, and promptly forgot what she had been talking about. Six missed calls from Guy. How could she have missed them? Oh, right, she had put her phone on silent before she went into the bookstore. Even when she texted Stephanie, she hadn't checked her missed calls, knowing at the time she could do nothing about them.

Guy started calling a little after ten, and then every hour. Whatever it was had to be urgent. All the same, she didn't feel comfortable returning his calls with all the listening ears around. Della preferred to keep her personal life private, which could be problematic with her mother.

Right now, she should say something since Stephanie focused on her. "Yes, I'll get right on it."

"I know you will. Why not have Elise help you since she's still here? I, on the other hand, need to go. Today I stayed due to unusual circumstances. Still, I'm not a full-time worker."

"I remember." The last time Della got pulled into sleuthing, Stephanie reminded her she needed extra help and not to depend on her as her Girl Friday. Here she was, depending on her like she promised she wouldn't. "I appreciate your staying today. It certainly wasn't my intention to take so long." She managed a sheepish smile. "I'd say it won't happen again, but I think we both know better."

"You bet." Stephanie crinkled her nose. "You and your mother can't stop sticking your spoon into whatever bubbles up in Owens."

Her stomach somersaulted at the insinuation. "We don't try to meddle. People ask us to help so what else can we do? Any decent human would do the same."

"Were you, Della Delacroix, specifically asked?" Stephanie folded her arms and leaned back against the wall. Her fixed expression announced she knew what she knew and wouldn't be persuaded otherwise.

"Okay, Lorna asked for my father. Since he'd dead, it's up to my mom and me. It isn't like we went looking for trouble."

"Yeah, right." Stephanie pushed off the wall. "Your father was a detective. You're not. I worry about you and your mother getting hurt."

"I worry about it, too." A little less than an hour ago, the subject absorbed her full attention. "The police apprehended the bad guys. Now all I have to do is figure out this annoying banking glitch. Could be a mechanical issue or even some virus that's causing issues."

Della thought otherwise, but a computer virus, while harmful, didn't usually bash anyone over the head with a blunt object. Then there were Clarice's phone messages from high-end car dealers.

"You do know there are experts who can handle this sort of issue."

Della bobbed her head in agreement, hoping the conversation would end so she could step into the tiny restroom and call Guy. After six unanswered calls, he might even rate a personal visit, but first, she needed to find out the nature of the issue. "I'd like to talk to one, but first, I need to pinpoint the problem. Experts don't show up when it's convenient. They have to be notified."

"You're going to notify them?"

"Good heavens, no. Not sure who to call. I'm hoping to solidify my theory first before contacting anyone. No worries, I'll be safe. The most dangerous activity I have coming up is the wedding I'm overseeing for Deborah Mifflin."

"Now that doesn't sound right." Stephanie rolled her eyes. "No one has ever accused Deborah of being helpful or considerate. I'll feel better for your sake when this is over."

"Me, too. I'd rather concentrate on my own clients as opposed to serving someone else's."

Stephanie pointed back to herself. "Repeat after me. I can't help you. I'm busy. A simple *no* works, too. It's probably what all the other caterers said when Deborah hit them up."

Her employee made a valid point. Unfortunately, she felt sorry for Deborah with her father having had a heart attack and all. Then again, what if her father wasn't ill at all?

"Okay." She held up both hands as if surrendering. "I will not be a pushover next time. If it looks like I am, you have permission to remind me."

"Oh, trust me. I will." Stephanie's hand went back to her hair and pulled off the tie before grabbing her jacket. She shot one arm and then the other into the sleeves as she spoke. "I'll also remind you that you told me to." She held up one hand. "I'm off."

Della held up her hand in farewell and waited for two heartbeats before heading into the bathroom. Possible scenarios crowded her mind, including the man contracting an incurable disease, the restaurant burning down, or being confronted with a wife he considered dead. The last one came from a Doris Day movie. Her mother happened to be a big fan.

Inside the tiny room, she turned on the light which also activated the exhaust fan. She called and waited for three rings before Guy picked up.

"Hello?"

"Hey, you called?"

"Are you in a wind tunnel or what?"

Not wanting to mention calling from the bathroom, Della switched off the fan and light. "Can you hear me better?"

"Yes. All day long, I kept calling. I was starting to worry about you."

"You're not the only one."

"Huh?"

"Never mind. What's so important?"

Silence. Then he said, "You're going to kill me. You must think I'm the most stupid man on God's green earth."

None of it sounded like the restaurant burning down or an incurable disease. "Your wife, the one you thought lost at sea, just returned?"

"What?"

Confusion was evident in his voice. Well, that meant no missing wife or anyone in the family who watched movies about missing wives showing up at inopportune times. "Forget it. Trying to be funny."

"Yeah, you won't be laughing once I tell you."

"Tell me, then."

He cleared his throat, which the phone magnified or sounded like it did. "I was talking to my sister. She asked who I was bringing, and I mentioned you."

"Should I worry about your sister?"

"Not too much. She might try to tell you embarrassing stories about when I was young."

"Sounds fun. Somewhat worrisome for you. I'm still not getting it."

"She reminded me the wedding is this Saturday."

"This Saturday?"

Her shock intensified when Elise swung open the door and shrieked. Equally surprised, Della yelped.

Her employee, now red-faced, gasped. "I didn't expect anyone in the bathroom since the door was unlocked."

There was not much Della could do but step out of the room and allow her employee to have it. With her phone cradled to her ear, she drifted into the front of the shop and inspected the countertops and tables to make sure they'd been cleaned.

Not certain she heard right, she asked, "You did say *this* Saturday?"

"Was that you who screamed?"

"No, although I may have yelped, it was Elise, my employee, who shrieked."

"Since you didn't scream, I guess it's safe to say this Saturday then. When I was talking to my sister, I mentioned I'd ordered a suit for the wedding. She asked me if I expected to get it in time. I told her a month was plenty of time. That's when she mentioned it was tomorrow. Wanting to prove her wrong, I grabbed the invitation and noticed they had all this fancy writing. The date was a curly 2, not a 3, which it looked like." His voice dropped a little. "Should I even ask if you'd be free tomorrow?"

Some of those fonts could be tricky. The number of times he called, along with his tone, bore witness to his panicked state. If she hadn't said yes to Deborah Mifflin, she'd be free. "No, I'm not. I'm so sorry."

"Don't apologize. It's on me." He audibly exhaled. "Of course, when I show up alone, my sister will tease me about misplacing my date."

For a moment, Della played with the idea of abandoning the reception she'd agreed to oversee. The only problem with that was it would wreck her catering reputation because Deborah would put the word out Della couldn't be trusted. "Let me know at least two weeks in advance if you come across any more wedding invites."

"You're not mad at me?"

"Simple mistake. Not sure why I should be mad about that."

"You're a peach."

It was not the first time she'd been called that. "Yeah, that's what I've been told. Have a good time at the wedding. You can tell me about it later."

They both said their goodbyes and hung up.

For some reason, they just kept missing each other. The thought depressed her. Good thing she'd be whipping up some extra rich, chocolate frosting. Chocolate made any problem not as bad.

# CHAPTER TWENTY-FIVE

T HE STEAMY HEAT from the convection ovens saturated the bakery kitchen with the high notes of lemon and heavier notes of chocolate. Della maneuvered the spatula underneath the golden oatmeal cookie chock-full of raisins. She promoted the cookie as an alternative to a bowl of oatmeal, which made it a breakfast cookie. All her cookies delivered fabulous taste and just the right amount of crunch. Even though most people swore ingredients mattered most, Della knew baking mattered just as much.

Excited for the prospect to showcase her cupcakes at the wedding, Della arrived at the bakery extra early. Technically, Deborah's team bore the responsibility for loading the van, but Della would be on hand all the same. Many a reception went awry when the simplest thing had been forgotten, such as the matches to light the Sterno cups for the chafing pans. That never happened with her since she was a planner surrounded by equally detail-oriented people and the fact that her mother could pull almost anything out of her purse. The woman missed her calling. She'd never attended the game show that paid cash for strange items in purses.

A few morning workers would be in looking for their coffee and pastries. Technically, she didn't open until eight-thirty on Saturday, but she made an exception for those nose-to-the-grindstone types. She'd better start the coffee before they slipped in for their morning java and treat. As she bustled around, regret rode her shoulders, whispering into her ear that she and Guy were not meant to be. After all, should it be this much trouble to date? They saw each other weekly in their exchange of cookies for buns as well as spoke on the phone.

Their devotion to starting businesses absorbed most of their time. When she wasn't inserting truffles inside of chocolate cupcakes for a luxurious surprise, she found herself involved in one of Owens' many issues. They never, necessarily, started out as a criminal activity but transformed the more she and her mother dug into them. How many questionable activities were never investigated, and the perpetrators got away with it?

The thought reminded her of her latest theory. "I need to call Mom," she spoke the words as the back door opened, revealing Mabel Delacroix.

"Here I am. What do you need to tell me?"

Della blinked. Her mother hadn't been on the schedule to work. "What are you doing here?"

"What a greeting. You should say how wonderful to see me. How grateful you are to have a mother who's an early bird or something like that. I wouldn't be opposed to best mother in the world." She chuckled at the last sentiment as she hung up her car coat on the hook. "Besides, I thought you might need help. Maybe you're a little rattled handling the Mifflin event."

Was she rattled? She audibly exhaled as if she'd been holding her breath forever. "Don't know. I'm okay handling my own events that *I* can organize. Someone else's is full of unknowns. Besides, it's Deborah Mifflin. Everyone knows her and most of Owens uses her if they can afford her. My goal with Cupid's Catering Company is to provide a nice option for the less well-heeled members of the community."

"You're doing a great job." Mabel stowed her purse and sniffed the air. "Coffee ready?"

"Almost." She probably inherited her love of coffee from both parents. Her mother delicately wrapped a turban-style hat over her short curls. Most of the time, those with long hair tied it back, and shorter haired folks like her mother settled for a hairnet or a ball cap. "What are you putting on your head?"

"Coiffure Cure. It keeps your hairdo fresh even when you sleep. I would have worn it in the car, but when you do something like that, inevitably you're pulled over. Just like you in the clown costume."

The memory elicited a groan. "Don't remind me. It's something I'd like to forget. Stephanie's hinted at Deborah Mifflin using me, but I might rather be used than don the clown outfit again. Why do you need a fresh hairdo anyhow? Hot date?"

"Nope. Not unless you count Vanessa as my date. We're attending the wedding you're catering."

"What?" While she knew her mother and her friend, Clarice, crashed weddings, she didn't know Vanessa had become part of the practice. "Crashing?"

"Mercy, no. We got a regular invitation, all fancy font and all. So elaborate it was almost unreadable. Luckily, I took calligraphy down at the art store and could decipher it."

A suspicion took form in her head as her mother continued to speak.

"Vanessa and I attended school with the bride's mother. Most weddings are more about the parents providing a decent party for their friends to show off how well they're doing. They know it'll be compared to previous weddings the guests attended. It makes me wonder why Deborah is bowing out on showing up."

That one Della could answer. "Her father had a heart attack, and she needs to fly to Arizona, I think, to make sure he's doing okay."

"Ha!" Her mother smirked "Wish you had talked to me before taking the job. She'll have to fly a lot farther than Arizona to see her dad. He's been dead five years or more. I would have clued you in if I'd known that was the excuse she gave. Clarice has spotted the woman in Columbus with a particular gentleman. Apparently, a romantic getaway trumped an actual business engagement. It must be serious if Deborah wants to avoid the wedding reception. She strikes me as a woman who never voluntarily gives control to others."

As gossip went, Clarice served as a reliable source. Not knowing what she might be walking into bothered Della, but it had to be better than dressing up as a clown for a child's birthday party. Did kids even want clowns for their birthdays? Small kids wanted bounce houses. Older children preferred parties at venues such as laser tag, a go-kart course, or even a theme park—definitely not a clown torturing balloons into unrecognizable animals.

All she could do was show up early and get her ducks in a row. Promptness and organization served as the base of her skill set. "Not much I can do about it now. Maybe she wanted to keep her man under wraps."

"That, I believe." Her mother gave a derisive snort as she washed her hands. "Probably doesn't want anyone mentioning she's had about as many husbands as Elizabeth Taylor. At her age, a man could accept a previous husband, even two. Any more than that just makes you look odd. He'd have to wonder if she's in the business of killing them or driving them off."

As a child, she'd thought Owens was the typical small town until she became an adult and the facets of the town came to light. "I didn't know that."

"No reason you should." Her mother opened the cabinet and removed her coffee cup. "I'll give the woman credit. She's always done it her way, never caring if a few people looked down their noses at her. That doesn't mean she's sweet or kind but more that she's the takes-what-she-wants type. That leads me back to why abandon her own catering assignment?"

Della lifted a tray of perfectly arranged cookies for the display case. "This time tomorrow, I'll be sleeping late, recovering from whatever surprises might be in store for me. All I can do is my job the best I can."

"Ah, sweetie, you're so like your father. Let me grab some coffee and tell you what else Clarice found out."

With her mother's friend collecting gossip, it made her wonder how the woman managed a personal life of her own. Her mother assured her Clarice enjoyed unbridled popularity since people wanted to know what she knew.

Della slid in the cookie trays as her mother poured herself a cup of joe. A couple of her early-bird customers delayed her from finding out what other gossipy tidbits Clarice had unearthed.

Her mother waited for the last customer to leave before speaking. "Clarice stopped by the car dealerships first. It's to be expected. She wanted to know if someone is pretending to be her. Turns out an actual woman wearing a black sheath, sunglasses, and slicked back hair stopped by both dealerships, claiming to be Clarice.

Anyhow, one of the salespeople was posing with a couple she'd just sold an S class sedan. It was her fiftieth sale. In the background of the picture is the imposter."

"Did they give her a copy?"

"Of course."

"Weird that the imposter would leave Clarice's phone number."

"Oh, no. The salesmen figured that out on their own. Clarice must be one of the few people who still has a land line. Said she needs it for work."

An actual person running around town pretending to be Clarice rather messed with her bank theory. She shook her head in confusion. "It makes me wonder what the imposter's plan was. Can you buy a car with a credit card?"

Her mother grimaced. "Interest rate is terrible, but some people do. She could have put a down payment on a fraudulent card and drove off with her purchase, but lucky for Clarice, the woman wanted to shop around a bit."

The incredible brass of the imposter awed Della in a creepy way. "Did Clarice find out anything else?"

"Oh yes," Her mother bobbed her head. "She asked around and not everyone is experiencing trouble with their banking funds or debit cards, just the folks who bank at—"

"Owens Fidelity." Della finished her mother's statement much to her open-mouthed parent's surprise.

"How did you know?"

She held up one finger. "I have a theory. It would depend on the bank having the most accounts and most money. More accounts mean small changes are not noticeable immediately."

Her mother shook her head before Della could finish her theory.

How in the world would she know what Della was going to say before she said it? "What is it, Mother?"

"Internal audits. They do it every year. I think the government, or someone, insists on it. I've heard Frank, the manager at my bank, complain about the time and man-hours it wastes."

Well, that shot another hole into her theory. Della got her own cup of coffee as the wheels in her mind kept spinning. "Who does the audit?"

"I assume bank staffers. It must be rather like balancing an over-sized checkbook. I don't think outside audits happen until there's suspicion that all is not what it seems." Mabel took a sip of her coffee and arched her eyebrows. "What do you think?"

"During an audit, they examine numbers on spreadsheets. Numbers can be changed to reflect whatever the depositor thinks is in their account. They don't find out otherwise until they attempt to withdraw that amount. You can have auditors believing everything is fine, or you could have the culprits serving as the auditors."

Her mother put down her coffee cup and tapped her temple. "My goodness, you just might have something there. I need to pass this on to Frank, but the bank office is closed on Saturday."

That meant another weekend would pass, allowing whoever treated the bank customer's money as their own a few more days to play. "It makes me wonder if the guilty party hasn't left already. People are complaining."

The display door creaked as Mabel opened it and selected a lemon drop cookie. Her eyelids closed after she bit into it. After chewing, she sighed. "These are so good. The extra weight I've put on is directly related to these and your fudgy brownie cookies." She waved the rest of the uneaten cookie as she spoke. "Don't worry about Frank. I'll see him at the wedding. He should know if any employees have recently departed."

Her mother made it sound like one of the employees faked their own death to throw off suspicion. This certainly would be a wedding to remember.

# CHAPTER TWENTY-SIX

EVEN THOUGH DEBORAH hadn't mentioned any attire, Della felt she had to wear her Cupid's Catering Company uniform of black pants, a T-shirt, and the black cook's apron emblazoned with the logo of flying cupids. After all, she wasn't Deborah's employee, but a fellow caterer. She stood near the van, supervising the loading while secretly admiring the vehicle. Instead of the usual open area most cargo vans boasted, this had shelves and hooks to lock down equipment. With the rentals Della used, a sharp turn could send scalloped potatoes for thirty skittering across the van floor, which is why they now packed the food in boxes and allowed enough time to drive like a granny searching for an address. A touch of envy—no, make that a streak about a foot wide—came over Della. Someday she'd have her own catering van.

The crew worked efficiently, familiar with the drill. Truthfully, Della hadn't known what to expect, even though any crew who worked with Deborah should be reasonably seasoned. She added three long bakery boxes that included her double chocolate cupcakes to the back of the van and watched as they were secured.

Her original plan had been to follow the van, but it felt a little too stand-offish to her. "Who's riding in the van?"

The male servers exchanged glances and shrugged. "Yolanda drives. We drive separately because we leave once the van is loaded after the reception. No reason to come back here."

*Besides the obvious one to unload the van and clean up*, Della thought. She turned toward Yolanda, the forty-something, ebony-skinned woman who had the height and attitude to be a model. She told Della, "That's what they do."

"Meaning there's room for me to ride with you?"

Yolanda did a double take. "You want to ride with me?"

"Yes." Della wondered if she should have asked. It could be the woman enjoyed the quiet before the bustle of the reception.

"All right, then."

She gestured for her to get in, which Della did. The servers climbed into two smaller cars.

Yolanda programmed the address into her phone and attached it to the dashboard with a sticky pad. "I've been to this church before, but the app lets me know if there are any traffic issues. The boys follow me, so I need to get it right. Why did you decide to ride with me?"

"Why not?" Della shrugged. "I always ride with my crew, what little there is."

"That's nice." She started the van and waited as it warmed up.

"It's all I know. Speaking of knowing, tell me about the reception, the bride—all the must knows. I prefer to be prepared."

Yolanda gave a low chuckle that positively sounded evil. "You need the inside info. It's only fair to know what hot potato you're getting stuck with. First of all, only those who can afford Deborah Mifflin use her catering. She's considered the best. Our precious bride and anxious mother of the bride have been a bit demanding. I would have sworn they were trying out for a reality show. Brides Go Wild or Godzilla Meets Bridezilla. The venue has been changed three times. Even the date of the wedding was changed, which is why you're here. Apparently, my boss had other plans for this weekend, and it didn't include listening to complaints about the napkins being pink, not rose."

"Demanding bride. I've dealt with a few. Got it."

"Good thing you wore your own outfit. That way you can honestly say you don't work for Deborah Mifflin Catering. Tell them you're making a note of something or whatever. It doesn't matter. No matter how hard they rant about the chicken being dry or the glasses not being sparkly enough, they won't get one red cent back. Deborah doesn't do refunds."

"Good to know. Caterers really can't cancel at the last minute, especially after the food has been purchased and cooked."

"Not the last minute." Yolanda offered as she shifted into drive. "We had a wedding called off six months in advance. The groom was killed in a motorcycle accident. The deposit wasn't returned."

Harsh, but she stored the information under things to know. How did she know Yolanda wouldn't repeat whatever she said to Deborah? She didn't. Observation depended on listening more than talking. In this case, she needed to be familiar with how things worked with the crew. To do that, she needed to talk.

"Once we get there, is there anyone waiting to help you prep the food? Set it out and all?"

Yolanda gave a heavy sigh. "The boys are supposed to help. They don't do too much. They'll carry stuff, pass trays around, and smile at all the pretty girls. None of them have an eye for presentation and just plop stuff down on the buffet table like it was a church rummage sale. I have to do it all. I used to have a helper, but she got paid better and had more hours at the local burger place. Now it's just me."

"I'll help you. I can set up a decent buffet table, too. Part of my deal with Deborah was I could showcase one of my bakery specialties."

"Uh-huh, she mentioned it. Told me that was all on you. I'm not supposed to help you set up a table or anything."

"I wouldn't expect it."

The rest of the trip consisted of going over details of the meal and a few anecdotes about reception disasters. In no time, they arrived. The sky remained blue as they unpacked. Already, vehicles dotted the parking lot. A white, stretch limousine waited next to the church entrance. A local florist truck backed up to the other entrance and a frowning woman in a blue serge suit flew out of the church, shouting something as the workers unloaded potted palms.

"I hope there's another entrance," Della remarked, not wanting to get in the way of the florist or the angry woman.

"There is. We may have to walk a little more, but it will be good for Deborah's handsome servers. Another thing Deborah is known for is having the best-looking servers."

Della didn't have a clue people demanded that for a reception. Though not sure why it surprised her, it did. They slipped in using the handicapped ramp and walked into a dark reception hall. Della located the lights and switched them on. There were no tables set up, no decorations, nothing. Della turned to address Yolanda. "Are you sure we are supposed to set up here?"

A few of the servers already scrolled through their phones. One offered, "This is the address on my work assignment."

The other three agreed.

Yolanda pointed upward. "Remember the angry lady in the blue suit?"

"Yeah." Della had a feeling she wasn't going to like where this was going.

"Mother of the bride. Do you want to go ask her if we should be elsewhere?"

That would be a giant *no*. Apparently, all the changes resulted in a few things falling into the cracks. Time for her to oversee. "Okay. We got tables to set up. Eight chairs at each one. Enough room so people can pull out their chair and not hit the wait staff. We have two hundred guests, which means we need twenty-five rounds, two to three rectangular ones for the buffet, another two for the bridal party, and a rounder for the cake."

Grumbling came from the servers. "We don't do tables. We're waiters."

The first obstacle. Della lifted her chin, narrowed her eyes, and smiled—not a sweet smile, but rather a mysterious, menacing one. "Today, you do. Who knows? I may give such a wonderful report on all of you working so hard that you may get a very special surprise later."

A couple of the guys started rolling tables and setting them up. The other two were slower, but they were moving, which was a positive.

"Let's go turn on the stoves and find some carts. It will probably take them most of the setup time to get the tables ready."

The two of them located a pair of stainless-steel carts that could handle the ramp and wheeled them to the van. As Yolanda passed Della a tray of chicken breasts, she remarked, "You know Deborah won't give the servers anything extra. They stay until they find a better job, and then they vanish, too."

"I guessed as much." Della loaded one cart and then pulled the other one up. "I did say *may* twice."

"That you did."

Back inside, Della locked the doors to the reception hall as they bustled around trying to pull things together. Having worked receptions before, she knew you had bored guests in search of snacks, children playing random games, and the occasional lovesick couple who wanted privacy. She didn't need any of them right now. The tables were soon set up and surrounded by the appropriate number of chairs.

Della tied tablecloths on and handed out stacks of plates to two servers. "Eight to a table, evenly spaced. Think of a person sitting in the chair."

The other snickering servers were given the salad and bread plates. Della darted back into a storage closet in search of decorations. She found Christmas ivy and holly wrapped around a red candle sitting on a mirrored square. It was workable only if she pulled off the ivy and holly. Abandoning the closet, she searched the next room which appeared to be an office of a sort. On top of a craft table sat boxes of hurricane lanterns with silk rosebuds circling the base and a single, white candle inside. They must be the decorations. Weird place to put them, though.

Candles lit, tables set, Della attended to her own display. She pulled the heart-strewn tablecloth that had *Cupid's Catering Service* on the hem all around it out of her bag. No signage. Just a tablecloth with a very minor message. Most would never read it. Using frames of various sizes, she created circles of cupcakes. It needed something more. Luckily, she brought it. Reaching into her bag, she pulled out her cupid statue and put it in the center of the table.

Yolanda came up beside her. "They look delicious."

Della handed her a cupcake. "You judge."

The woman bit into it, and her eyes widened with appreciation. She swallowed and asked, "What's the filling?"

"A truffle melted by the heat of the oven."

"Perfect." She finished off the cupcake and licked her fingers. "The hall looks all right, considering what we had. We can probably have the servers unlock the doors since we're ready."

The doors opened with a click and guests poured in from the wedding ceremony. They came in talking and searching the tables for name cards. Finding none, they sat where they pleased. A few tilted chairs against the table to save chairs for others.

Della mentally repeated to herself *not my circus, not my clowns.* So far, no one had much to say positive about Deborah. Could she have set Della up to fail with an unprepared reception area and handsome servers who did little more than circle, fill glasses, and point the way to the restrooms?

Della heard a familiar voice before she saw Guy. He entered the reception area with an attractive woman on his arm. Her heart took a stumble seeing how fast he'd replaced her as a date. The woman giggled and pinched Guy. It was peculiar behavior, which might not result in a second date, which pleased Della.

As they drew closer, she could hear the woman. "Where is this mystery woman you were bringing? What did you do to scare her off?"

Were they talking about her? Della moved closer by straightening a spoon in the mashed potatoes. A hungry guest inquired if it was time to eat. "Soon. Show me where you're sitting, so I make sure to signal your table first."

"You're my kind of girl!" the man cried with enthusiasm, causing Guy and the woman to turn.

If Della bet on Guy being shocked or embarrassed, she'd be out of money. The man grinned from ear to ear.

"Here she is!" Guy announced and moved to stand beside Della, wrapping an arm around her shoulder. "Della, I'd like you to meet my sister, who is certain I couldn't land a date on my own."

His sister. It made sense. She shot the woman a relieved smile. "He can get a date for the wedding, if the wedding doesn't change dates."

"Tell me about it. I'd love to grill you, but I can see you're working."

"Make your way to the table with cupids on the side and try one of my cupcakes. Everything else is Deborah, but I brought the cupcakes."

Guy offered. "We'd better hurry before they disappear. They will. I guarantee it."

It was nice he thought so well of her skills. Before she could bask in the praise, other familiar voices sounded—one being her mother's. Vanessa and her mother trailed a distinguished gentleman going silver at the temples.

Her mother's voice carried, "Frank, you've got to listen to me. Something weird is going on at your bank. Money is getting moved around. I can look at my account and have plenty of money, then go to the ATM and be told I'm out of funds."

The man looked pained, probably not so much over discussing business at a personal affair, but at the possibility of someone overhearing. "You probably just overdrew funds. That's all. Not surprised with Kenneth being gone."

Talk about a warning shot over the bow. Della took a deliberate step back while Vanessa moved closer not to miss anything and added, "Tell him about the fifty-two customers you found so far who complained about their balances always changing. Never huge amounts, but being short ten, twenty dollars every month."

Frank gulped. "You've been talking to customers?"

"They've been talking to each other. Let me tell you, they aren't happy. You need an outside audit because something fishy is going on." Mabel placed one hand on her hip. "That remark you made about Kenneth being gone was a low one. I have always balanced the checkbook to the penny. That's why I know something is wrong."

"You're talking nonsense. I just had an internal audit. Kathy, my wife's cousin, did it. She's here. Let me get her. You'll see."

He disappeared into the throng of people, giving Della doubts he'd return—maybe for the buffet, but not to continue the conversation.

Her mother moved closer and asked, "What should we say to Kathy?"

"Tell her the movie plot about the woman taking money from bank customers. Ask her expert opinion on if it could happen and then judge her reaction."

Her mother nodded her head at the same moment the blue-serge-suited woman walked in. She glanced around the room at the happy guests and attractive tables. Coming closer, she asked, "Where's Deborah?"

That was the question of the day. Della stepped forward and said, "Family emergency. She asked me to oversee the reception. Della Delacroix from Cupid's Catering Service."

"Family emergency, huh?" The woman turned slowly, taking in the room. "You did okay. Where's the tacky photo cubes my daughter put together for the table decorations?"

"I never saw them."

The woman winked. "Good answer. You make the food?"

"Only the double chocolate cupcakes on the table with cupids on the side."

The mother of the bride wandered away without saying anything else, which could be a blessing. Frank returned with his grip on a slightly familiar-looking woman near forty, sporting a burgundy rinse and tiara. She resisted coming with him. Someone else might not think it signaled guilt, but Della sensed the buffet table could be in danger, remembering the takedown and knocked over tables at the bookstore. It looked like a scene in the making to her. She cocked her head in her mother's direction. Thankfully, Mabel understood the need to back away from the buffet line and closer to the doors. Wanting to distract with food, she signaled her hungry friend first, who practically galloped to be first in the buffet line.

Della announced in a raised voice that she'd go to each table to notify them when to line up. The servers would be circling with drinks. She carried a tiny triangle and mallet in her hand to signal each table. Hopeful diners half-raised in their seats as she moved closer. An accidental ting sent up a table sooner than she'd liked, but they'd survive.

Clarice came down the stairs and surveyed the room, and when she spotted Mabel, hurried over to join her. Even if Della didn't make it close enough to the resistant cousin, she'd have reliable sources.

As she drew closer, Kathy's face flushed as she demanded, "Who said something about my accounting?"

Giggling carried through the open door as a slender female with a slicked back chignon and a glittery sheath clung to the arm of a much younger man. Her gaze rested on her date and not on the woman twisting in Frank's grip until said woman growled. "Jenny, you rat! You're the problem! You ruined everything with your greedy ways and your expensive boy toy."

Della's hand hovered inches from the triangle as she took in the scene. She inhaled deeply as her mind spun out various scenarios, with most of them featuring overturned tables and brawling wedding guests sporting globs of macaroni and cheese from the spilt food. Suddenly, remembering to exhale, she let out her breath in a gust as she determined to protect her buffet line. Sure, she might not be the official caterer, but people would remember her being there. Her mallet wielding hand failed to cover her Cupid's Catering logo on her shirt. People would remember.

Meanwhile, Jenny froze and then turned slowly, blinked once, and made a tsking sound. "The poor woman is crazy." She pressed her hand to her chest. "She mistook me for someone else."

The words and tone caused a series of turned heads and whispers, with a few even standing to see better. A few inquiries sounded against the clink of china.

"What's happening?"

"Do you know her?"

A laugh floated from one of the tables, along with an undecipherable sentiment.

Not everyone found the situation amusing. Clarice's tensed shoulders and fisted hands telegraphed her mood. Intimidating in her tall heels, she stepped forward and cleared her throat.

"I didn't. Just the opposite. You've been busy impersonating me all over town and even ruining my travel plans. We're talking." She latched onto the woman, dragging her off to the side. The boy toy date vanished into the crowd.

Caught up in the drama, Della realized she hadn't rung the triangle. Darting to the closest table, she tinged it and then hurried to the next one. By the time she'd circled the room, Frank and Cousin Kathy had vanished, and her buffet line remained intact. There was no sign of Clarice or the imposter she'd caught.

ALMOST AN HOUR later, most of the tables had been cleared and the plates packed away when the music started. Guests circled the floor, clapping softly as the bride and groom danced. Parents of both the bride and groom joined in, and then others as Della watched.

Guy appeared by her side and held out his hand.

"I'm working."

"One dance and not even a full one at that."

She took his hand, let him lead her onto the floor, and danced to the bride's chosen song, *At Last*, sung by Etta James. Thinking a woman who chose the song wasn't all bad, Della rested her cheek on Guy's shoulder as they slowly twirled across the floor. In fact, her brush with Bridezilla and the mother of the bride went very well. It was a very good night, indeed, and definitely better than Kathy and Jenny's.

# EPILOGUE

ELLA LIFTED ANOTHER tray of double chocolate cupcakes from the oven to cool. "This is my sixth batch today."

"And will be sold out by noon," Stephanie predicted and then grinned. "I'm sure one less won't hurt."

"Go ahead." She smiled at her employee. "It's the least I can do, considering the uptick in our business. I can't wait until Mom shows. She told me on the phone she knows the low down about Owens Fidelity."

"Talk about odd." Stephanie bit into her cupcake, chewed, and swallowed before continuing. "I got an apology form letter from Owens Fidelity, and I don't even bank there."

"They sure got that done in a hurry, and I think they sent it out to everyone. Basically, something bad happened, don't leave us, we'll make it right, without saying exactly what they will do."

"Yeah, it was something like that. Whatever happened with the reception you did for Deborah? Did she shaft you? Try to embarrass you?"

Had Deborah tried to trick her? She wrinkled her nose as she pondered the possibility. "It's hard to say. Turns out the mother of the bride had asked two teenage cousins to help set up the reception hall. They blew it off, so dumping that on me wasn't a set up."

She couldn't put that on Deborah's shoulders. When it came to unpaid help, a person could only expect so much. In the end, Della got paid, and her cupcakes became an overnight success. "No, none of the above. I think she wanted to sneak away with her boyfriend but didn't want anyone to know. On the positive side, I think I made a good impression on everyone. I know I'll never be Deborah Mifflin."

Mabel entered through the backdoor as Della finished her sentence. She gave a little huff and wrinkled her nose. "Why would you want to be?" She winked, then said, "Della Delacroix is pretty special."

"Thanks, Mom." Her mother always knew what to say. "I'll wait for you to get your coffee, and then I want to know everything."

"I had some coffee already. Not as good as yours, but I knew you were waiting." She hung up her coat, pulled up a stool, and pointed to a cupcake. "I'll take one of those and one of those little bottles of milk."

Della pulled a milk bottle out of the fridge that would suit a kids' drive-thru meal and placed it in front of her mother. "Glass?"

"No, I'm good." She smirked and then reached for a cupcake. "First, I'll tell you what I got from Delores down at the station. Can't say too much about Clarice's part of the story. She does love telling it on her own." She held up one finger. "Before you ask, she's coming by for a summary before she goes to the dentist."

Her mother enjoyed a bite of cupcake and washed it down with a swig of milk. "Okay, girls, here's what I know. Both Jenny and Kathy were booked on embezzlement and the cops are still looking into other charges. The two turned on each other like those Siamese fighting fish. Apparently, Kathy, the adult daughter of the woman who covered the bounced check, really couldn't act to superior to her sister-in-law who bungled the checkbook now and then. Could be the sister-in-law suffered more money withdrawn than other customers experienced. Possibly recognizing her poor math skills, the poor dear never complained. Most hadn't mentioned missing a five here, a ten there, each month. Even if they had, the bank would assume the customer messed up the balance. Kathy had up to a hundred thousand in a side account. Forensic accounting is going to investigate that. There may be money hidden elsewhere."

"What about Jenny?" Stephanie asked.

"Turns out she figured out what Kathy was doing. Sort of amazing as a new hire that she noticed when none of the regular employees did. Then again, not too surprising when you consider Jenny's colorful past."

Mabel put a finger up to her lips as if hushing herself. "I don't want to get into Clarice's story. Sufficient to say she promised to keep quiet if she got a cut, but she didn't want to wait around years like Kathy, which resulted in more obvious issues. They were moving money around. They'd take fifty from my account and by the time I made a fuss about it, they'd moved fifty back. They would tell me I was confused or some other nonsense when I mentioned it. No overdrawn fees served as my tipoff. Their best accounts included saving accounts of hardcore savers who never used them and recently deceased customers who surprisingly died with no money to their names. Kathy's formula kept the numbers the same while extracting money, but only in small amounts. No one became too concerned with little amounts."

A heavy pounding on the back door resulted in Mabel stopping her narrative to yell, "It's open, Clarice. Come on in."

The woman hurried in with her parka half-zipped, revealing the scrubs underneath. "I'm here and wanted to give my side of the tale. I know Mabel probably told you about Kathy and how she was nickel and diming everyone, but no one had a clue Jenny—not her real name—has made a practice of inserting herself in places where she can get vital information about folks and their money. Her specialty is…" Clarice held up both hands. "…wait for it."

She grinned and then said, "Impersonating people. She's a bold one. Not content with skimming off a few dollars here or there or opening a fake store account. Nope. She dolls herself up and heads out, seeing what she can get. I think at first she was feeling out the salespeople, seeing who'd do the least checking."

One of Della's hands went to her throat as she put two and two together. The woman going by Jenny had picked up the sweet girl at Della's only clown appearance. How horrible for the girl to be relocated, possibly in the middle of the night, just to keep ahead of the law. With any luck, the woman didn't have custodial rights. "Doesn't she have a little girl?"

Clarice sucked in her lips and then pulled out her phone and typed. "We will find out in a couple of minutes. Who wants to hear the rest of my story?"

Three hands went up.

"Good. You should. Turns out Jenny, who has many aliases, was featured on the podcast about weird crimes. Apparently about seven or eight years ago, she broke into some snowbird's house in Michigan while they were wintering in Florida. She used their house. Even had pizza delivered there. All sorts of stuff. The locals assumed she had to be a relative. Anyhow, once her photo showed up in the police database, people started IDing her." Clarice pointed a thumb to herself. "If it hadn't been for me, she'd have gotten away scot-free."

Della caught her mother's eyes. There was no need to mention that Clarice hadn't been the sole investigator. The woman in question glanced down at her phone. "There is a little girl, and her paternal grandmother, a retired teacher, is looking after her."

The thought pleased Della. Perhaps the girl would have a chance at a normal life. "Thanks for finding out."

"No problem. I gotta go. Getting my teeth whitened because I'm going to be on a true crime show. Woo-hoo."

They said their goodbyes to Clarice, who swept out of the kitchen. Stephanie regarded both Mabel and Della with a quizzical expression. "Why does she get to be on a true crime show?"

Mabel sighed. "It's because she wants to. I honestly think Kathy might have gotten away with it if Jenny hadn't figured it out and wanted a cut. Of course, Kathy could have vanished at any time, but she stayed for more money. Disappoints me."

Most of the conversation Della understood, but she lost her mother somewhere. "What disappoints?"

"The fact Kathy could wish me good morning when I entered the bank when all the while she was ripping me off. I'm also disappointed in myself that I never suspected."

Betrayal made you doubt yourself. "Don't blame yourself. You expect people to have the same principles as yourself. Most folks do. All we can do is live the best life possible. For me, it's make the best bakery treats possible. How about you?"

Mabel chuckled. "I'll be by your side, helping taste test your treats and possibly investigate things that don't smell right, if you know what I mean."

"I do know," Della agreed. "When it comes to sniffing out shenanigans of the felonious nature, you're a bloodhound."

"Aroo." Her mother tried to bay but instead, choked on the cupcake she'd just bitten into. A hearty slap on the back delivered by Della stopped the coughing. Her mother reached for the milk and emptied the bottle with a sigh. "I guess I'll settle for being able to catch a scent like a bloodhound and leave the baying to Tony."

On that, they all could agree.

## THE END

# Double Chocolate Deception Cupcakes

**Prep Time**: 15 mins

**Cook Time**: 25 mins

**Total Time**: 40 mins

**Servings**: 12 cupcakes

**Ingredients**

*For the cupcakes:*
- 1 cup (4 1/2 oz) all-purpose flour
- 1/2 cup (2 oz) Dutch-processed cocoa powder, sifted
- 1/2 teaspoon baking powder
- 1/4 teaspoon baking soda
- 1/4 teaspoon kosher salt
- 1 cup (4 oz) sugar
- 3/4 cup buttermilk
- 1/2 cup canola oil
- 2 large eggs
- 2 teaspoons vanilla extract

*For the frosting:*
- 8 ounces dark chocolate
- 1 tablespoon corn syrup
- 1/2 cup softened unsalted butter
- 1 1/2 to 2 cups powdered sugar
- 2 tablespoons Dutch-processed cocoa powder
- 4 to 6 tablespoons heavy whipping cream
- Pinch of kosher salt
- Chocolate sprinkles

**Method**
- Preheat the oven to 350°F:
- Line a muffin tin with 12 paper liners.

*Make the cake batter:*
- In a mixing bowl, whisk the flour, sifted cocoa powder, baking powder, baking soda, salt, and sugar together. In a large liquid measuring cup, whisk together the buttermilk, canola oil, eggs, and vanilla. Pour the buttermilk mixture into the dry ingredients and whisk until just smooth and combined.

*Bake the cupcakes:*
- Divide the batter evenly between the muffin cups. Bake in the preheated oven for about 25 minutes, or until the tops of the cupcakes spring back to the touch and a toothpick inserted in the center comes out clean.
- Remove from the oven and cool completely on a rack before frosting.
- Melt the chocolate for the frosting:
- Place the chocolate for the frosting in a glass measuring cup and melt in the microwave for 30-second intervals, stirring between each, until completely smooth. Stir in the corn syrup.
- Set aside to cool to room temperature

*Make the frosting:*
- In the bowl of a stand mixer, beat the butter until soft. Add 1 1/2 cups of powdered sugar and cocoa powder. Beat until combined; it may be crumbly, but that's okay. Beat in 4 tablespoons of the heavy cream and the salt and continue beating until the mixture smooths out.
- Beat in the room temperature chocolate and corn syrup into the mixture until smooth and incorporated. If needed, beat in additional powdered sugar and/or heavy cream to get a smooth and spreadable consistency that you like.
- Spread the frosting onto the cooled cupcakes using an offset spatula or butter knife, or transfer to a piping bag and pipe. Top with sprinkles if you want.

# Company Sheet Cake

**Prep Time**: 15 mins

**Cook Time**: 25 mins

**Total Time**: 40 mins

**Servings**: 36 servings

**Ingredients**

*For the cake:*
- 2 cups (8.8 ounces) all-purpose flour
- 2 cups (14 ounces) granulated sugar
- 1/2 teaspoon kosher salt
- 1 cup (8 ounces) unsalted butter
- 1 cup water
- 1/4 cup (1 ounce) natural unsweetened cocoa powder
- 1/2 cup buttermilk
- 2 large eggs
- 2 teaspoons vanilla extract
- 1/2 teaspoon baking soda

*For the frosting:*
- 3/4 cup (6 ounces) unsalted butter
- 5 tablespoons natural cocoa powder
- 1/2 cup milk, whole or 2 percent
- 1 teaspoon vanilla extract
- Pinch of kosher salt
- 3 cups (15 ounces) powdered sugar, sifted
- 1 cup chopped pecans (4.5 ounces)

## Method

- Preheat the oven and prep the pan:
- Preheat the oven to 350°F. Spray or butter a half-sheet pan (13x18 inches) and line the bottom with parchment.
- Combine the dry ingredients:
- Whisk the flour, sugar, and salt together in a large mixing bowl.

*Make the batter:*

- In a saucepan over medium-low heat, combine the butter, water, and cocoa powder. Whisk until melted and smooth, and then bring to a simmer. Once simmering, remove from the heat.
- Using a whisk or electric mixer, beat the hot cocoa mixture into the dry ingredients until combined. Beat in the buttermilk, eggs, and vanilla, followed by the baking soda until combined.

*Bake the cake:*

- Spread the batter into the prepared pan and bake for 25 to 28 minutes, or until a toothpick inserted in the center comes out clean.
- Remove from the oven and set the pan on a wire rack to cool briefly, about 5 to 10 minutes, while you make the frosting.

*Frost the cake:*

- As soon as the cake is done baking and on the cooling rack, combine the butter, cocoa, and milk for the frosting in a saucepan and bring to a boil. Remove from the heat and stir in the salt and vanilla. Beat in the powdered sugar with an electric mixer or by hand.
- Pour the hot frosting over the still-warm cake and spread evenly. Sprinkle the top with chopped pecans.
- Allow to set, then serve immediately or cool completely and cover to serve later. You can also wrap the cake well in foil or plastic wrap and freeze.

# TRIPLE CHOCOLATE CHEESECAKE

**Prep Time**: 60 mins

**Cook Time**: 60 mins

**Chill Time**: 12 hrs

**Total Time**: 14 hrs

**Servings**: 12 servings

Let the eggs and cream cheese come to room temperature before making this cheesecake.

You will also need to make this cake twenty-four hours before you want to serve it to allow adequate time to chill, and frankly, we all need a bit more chill time.

**Ingredients**

*For the crust:*
- 8 chocolate graham crackers, crushed (about 1 1/4 cups)
- 1/3 cup (66 g) sugar
- 1 tablespoon cocoa powder
- Pinch of kosher salt
- 4 tablespoons unsalted butter, melted

You can also substitute Keebler pre-made chocolate graham cracker crust.

*For the filling:*
- 8 ounces semi-sweet chocolate, chopped

- 1/3 cup heavy whipping cream
- 4 large eggs, room temperature
- 2 teaspoons vanilla extract
- 1/4 teaspoon kosher salt
- 3 (8 ounce) packages cream cheese, room temperature
- 1 1/4 cup (250 g) sugar
- 2 tablespoons cocoa powder

*For the ganache topping:*
- 3/4 cup heavy whipping cream
- 1 tablespoon corn syrup (optional)
- Pinch of kosher salt
- 8 oz semi-sweet chocolate, finely chopped
- 1 teaspoon vanilla extract

**Method**
- Preheat the oven to 350°F

*Make the crust:*
- In the bowl of a food processor fitted with the metal S-blade attachment, add the graham crackers. Pulse until they are ground fine like sand.
- Add the sugar, cocoa powder, and salt. Pulse 2 or 3 times until just combined. Pour melted butter around the bowl in a circle, pulse 4 or 5 times combine it. The mixture should clump a little bit, but may still look a little dry.
- Dump the mixture into the bottom of your ungreased springform pan. Use your fingers or the underside of a cup to press the mixture into the bottom of the pan, making it as even as possible.
- Place the crust in the oven and bake for about 8 to 10 minutes. Remove from oven to cool.
- Reduce the oven temp and melt the chocolate:
- Once the crust has baked, reduce the oven to 300°F.
- In a medium-sized, heavy-bottom saucepan set over low heat,

combine the chopped

- chocolate and 1/3 cup heavy cream. Stir continuously, for about 10 minutes.
- Once melted, remove from heat, and set aside. You will fold it into your filling later.

*Make the cheesecake filling:*

- In a small bowl or Pyrex measuring cup, gently beat the eggs, vanilla extract, and salt together with a fork. Set it aside.
- Using a stand mixer fitted with a paddle attachment (or a hand mixer set to low and a large bowl), add the cream cheese. Beat the cream cheese on low or stir speed until creamy, about 2 minutes. Scrape down the sides and bottom of the bowl.
- Beat again on low for about 1 minute. With the stand mixer still on low, slowly add the sugar and two tablespoons of cocoa powder. Stop the mixer. Scrape down the bottom and sides of the bowl. Beat for another minute or two until light and fluffy.
- With the mixture still on low, add the egg mixture, 1/3 at a time, scraping down the sides of the bowl after each addition.
- Pour the cooled, melted chocolate into the bowl of the stand mixer and (you guessed it!) beat on low for about a minute. Scrape down the sides and bottom of the bowl. Beat on low again for about 30 seconds, or until the chocolate is fully incorporated. Alternatively, you can fold in the chocolate using a spatula.

*Prepare the water bath and add the filling:*

- Wrap the outside of your springform pan in 3 layers of aluminum foil. Be careful not to tear or puncture the foil. Bring the foil all the way up the sides. Set it inside a roasting pan or a large Dutch oven.
- Pour the filling into a springform pan.
- Fill the roasting pan with warm water about halfway up the sides of the springform pan. Be careful not to splash any water into the cheesecake pan or inside the foil.

*Bake the cheesecake:*

- Put the pan in the oven and bake until the cheesecake is just barely set in the center, 55-65 minutes. It will still jiggle slightly, but shouldn't slosh in the center when moved.

*Let it cool, then chill:*

- Remove the roasting pan from the oven. Let the cake cool in the water bath for about an hour. Then remove it from the water bath and transfer it to a cooling rack on the counter for another hour. Finally, keep the cake in the springform pan, and let it chill, uncovered overnight in the fridge.

*Make the ganache:*

- Place chopped chocolate in a medium-sized bowl. In a small saucepan set over medium heat, add the heavy cream, corn syrup, and salt. Stir to combine and bring to a simmer.
- Pour the heated cream over the chopped chocolate. Don't stir. Let sit for 5 minutes, then add the vanilla. Use a spatula and stir gently to combine. Let the ganache cool at room temperature for 2 hours. Cover with plastic wrap and keep it in the fridge until you're ready to serve the cheesecake.

Coming October 2021

# Two Many Sleuths

## Book Twelve of
## The Painted Lady Inn Mysteries

A WEEK WITHOUT a murder or the mention of any crime made Donna Tollhouse Taber grin. She adjusted the car window clamps on the British flags, then stepped back, resting her hands on her lower back. "I think it's a nice touch."

Her detective husband, Mark, ran a hand through his salt and pepper hair. "I don't know." His face scrunched up. "It might be over the top. Howard doesn't strike me as the showy type. He keeps things low-key, a proper Brit."

Typical. Her husband thought he knew all about the neighbors over the pond due to an online relationship he'd struck with Scotland Yard detective Howard Dudley, when he previously researched diamonds and jewel heists. Never mind her husband hadn't put in the hours she had watching BBC mysteries and The Great British Baking Show. If Howard didn't appreciate her effort to welcome them, his wife, Elizabeth, certainly would. "A proper Brit might mention they don't go in for pomp and ceremony, but just look at the royal weddings. They go crazy about those."

"Well, you'd know more about that than me. All I can hope for is a nice quiet time with no murders. I told the station not to call me unless it's an emergency. A vacation is still a vacation even if I don't leave the state."

"The best thing to do is not answer your phone." Donna had doubts about her husband not getting pulled into a case. The Legacy police force numbered thirty-eight, six more than last year. Surely, they could handle anything that came up on their own. Still, she gave her husband a loving perusal. Mark had solved eleven murders—with her help, of course. It's no wonder they'd need their help.

"Can't do that. It's not like I'm a stock boy and when I'm missing the green beans don't get shelved on time."

"I know." Before he could start his usual rant about a law enforcement officer being a public trust, she held up one hand. "I know it's an honor protecting the citizens of Legacy, but you need to let someone else do it."

"You're right," Mark agreed as he swung open the car door. "Let's go get our guests."

His phone rang on cue and Donna recognized the station chime. Her eyes rolled up, knowing the inevitable outcome. Her husband answered the phone and muttered, "Sorry to hear that but I'm still on vacation. I have faith you can handle it."

Donna slid into her side of the car and popped her CD of favorite British ballads into the player before closing the door. She waited until her husband wiggled behind the steering wheel before asking. "What did they want?"

"Assistance on a case," he answered while backing out.

That much she could have guessed. "What kind of case?"

"Probable murder."

"Probable?" The word *probable* had little to do with *murder.* Premediated, self-defense, even accidental could pair up with murder. "What makes it probable?"

"Shot in the back of the head while gardening."

Good heavens! A person murdered while pulling weeds or deadheading roses. "How awful. Anyone I know?"

While all crimes should be regarded with horror and repulsion, knowing the victim made it somehow worse.

"Margery Baumgarten."

"Margery!" She pressed her hands over her heart. "I just saw her the other day at the friends of the library luncheon. She brought the tomato mozzarella salad. It could have done with a touch of dill, but I'm grateful I didn't mention it. I'd hate for that to be on her mind before being killed."

Mark put the car into drive. "It is just as well I'm not handling the case. It's always hard dealing with friends. Too many emotions can cloud your judgment."

"Well, we weren't super good friends. In a town the size of Legacy, I went to school with everyone my age. Sure, I do see Margery at many events."

A few blocks passed without talking while the strands of Barbara Allen swirled around them. The melancholic music got Donna thinking about Margery. They hadn't been good friends, but she knew of her and some of her trials. Her husband Jeff's wandering eye was known—at least to Donna. "Tell them to check out the husband."

"They always do," Mark answered without looking at her. "Standard procedure."

Donna harrumphed. Sure, all the police dramas looked at family members first. Enough cold cases illustrated forensic procedure failed to nail down the case even when everyone knew the spouse should be charged. The facts only came out a few decades later. An eyewitness who saw something, but was too scared to speak finally came forward, a piece of evidence unearthed in the victim's former home by new owners, or just a crackerjack detective who decided to wade through the cold case files. She had a crackerjack detective sitting right beside her. However, Donna didn't discount her own personal strings she could pull for information.

"I think you should do it. No one handles murder like you do."

"Donna," Mark protested, "Who didn't want me to take any cases? I think you told me not to answer the phone."

"That's before I knew it was Margery."

"Who isn't your close friend."

"That part is true, but I've known her for fifty years. We were in first grade together. I feel like I should do something."

"We're on our way to pick up Howard and Emily."

"I know. I fixed the flags on the car and picked the music." But it didn't feel right to let a former classmate go unavenged. Not that Donna would dress in black and strap a sword to her back in her hunt for the murderer. Justice would be the best form of vengeance. "You don't have to go full throttle. Just find out the facts, point out what they're not doing right."

"Ha! *That* would make me popular. You need to decide. I can work on the case or not."

If he did, it would leave her with sole hostess duties of the Scotland Yard detective and his wife. She did have the supplies for a proper British tea ready. "Well, knowing you and your great observation skills, you should have the case wrapped up in no time.

Remember that the husband, Jeff, is a real dog. Makes passes at all the women in town."

Mark looked away from the road to his wife and growled, "Did he make a pass at you?"

Truthfully, she couldn't remember him doing so, which stung her vanity, but he always preferred much younger females. "*All* the women," she emphasized.

"Ok then, not you," he concluded with a nod.

No one could get anything past Detective Mark Taber. They pulled up in front of the police station, where Mark exited with a quick kiss. "This shouldn't take long. See you soon."

Donna took her place behind the wheel. While small talk wasn't her forte, surely, she could locate two foreign tourists, drive them back to the inn, serve them tea, and tuck them up in their room. By that time, Mark should be back.

# Author Notes

*Cupid Catering Company* is my first catering cozy mystery series. I've spent a great deal of my life cooking with family and for work. The possibility of a mother and daughter running a catering business appealed. Like all families, there would be some issues on which they didn't hold the same views. While daughter, Della, may not always agree with her mother, Mabel, she is respectful of her parent. The two genuinely love and look out for each other. For a change, the characters aren't based on anyone in my family, but the cooking is.

In **Double Chocolate Deception,** I used actual crimes. One even happened to me, a few decades ago. It just goes to show life is often stranger than fiction. Next time, you hear about a weird crime, there will be a writer somewhere saving it to their Pinterest board as a possibility for their next mystery.

The culinary aspects of the novel are courtesy of my grandmother plus my own experiences. My grandmother taught herself to cook and became quite well known for her pies. This talent kept her family fed since she spent her early morning hours at a bakery making bread, cookies, donuts, and pies for the day. I on the other hand worked in dietary at a local nursing home where I sometimes cooked for three hundred plus people. It became a running joke that I couldn't make anything for less than a hundred folks.

The recipes in this book rely heavily on chocolate—which is always my favorite ingredient. Writing this book resulted in much baking, eating, and possibly five extra pounds. I only hope it's five.

I love to hear from and meet readers. In the meantime, stay in touch via my newsletter. Sign up at www.morgankwyatt.com.

Subscribers find out about exclusive freebies, contests, and personal appearances.

If you feel like writing a review, please do.

*Reading takes you to your happy place. We need happy moments now more than ever.*

*MK Scott*
*www.morgankwyatt.com*

www.ingramcontent.com/pod-product-compliance
Lightning Source LLC
Chambersburg PA
CBHW050741230626
47052CB00004BA/928